Fun

BK Wells

www.bkwells.com

Funny Money

BK Wells

Copyright © 2021 BK Wells

Published by Wavin' Raven

Cover design by Usman

ISBN: 978-1-953531-04-9

First Printing: March 2021

Table of Contents

Chapter 1
Gimme A Break

I was in the bathroom, which was a dump, though I wasn't taking a dump, just a whiz. The bathroom was incredibly gross, though I had worked at Gimme A Brake for almost a month and I suppose I was used to the disgusting john. I was the only person in the joint who had female plumbing, and I guess the guys didn't mind that the toilet seat was covered in grease, or that oily filth was smeared all across the seat and that all things foul on Planet Earth were attached to the base; also the lid was crusty with dried-up human fluids. It was icky. I tried to hover and pee, but I just didn't have the leg strength or balance and fell onto the horrifying, cruddy plastic.

I hated this place. And I could only hide out in the bathroom for so long. Sooner or later, Sammy would come looking for me. The only thing I liked about this place was the money, oh, and it wasn't enough money. I don't know why I had decided to live in one of the world's most expensive cities. A lot of times I thought I should just move to someplace with a low cost of living, like Bumfuck, Wyoming, but y'know, murder. Those rednecks would kill me before I walked to the end of the block. They would shoot, stab, and poison me the minute I opened my smart little mouth and said, "Well hello, you stupid bumpkins!"

I looked at myself in the mirror, while the single bare lightbulb blazed above. Man, I looked like shit. I was only in my thirties, but I didn't have bags under my eyes, I had a complete set of luggage. It wasn't like I was drinking a lot or something, I just looked like hell. Then I realized it wasn't the reflection, it wasn't my ugly mug that was so frightening, it was my essence. That's what was scary. Like when people say, "She's beautiful... on the inside!" Me? I was hellish on the inside, and it shined through.

Okay, I don't know what was going on. I don't know why I did it, but I had a small wrench in my pocket, and I took it out. I had stared at myself for about eleven seconds and I couldn't take one more. I took the wrench and I smacked it against the mirror, and it made a metallic sound as it broke into about seven big pieces; a couple of them fell in the sink. For a second, I thought about the seven years of bad luck. But could things get worse than they already were? Oh, I had already learned that was the wrong question to ask.

Anyway, the mirror... it happened so fast; I don't even know that I thought about it. I just did it. Then, like a million other times in my life, I was faced with how I was gonna get out of it. I washed my hands off, being careful not to slash my wrists on the mirror shards, then I pulled a paper towel off the roll. The paper towels were disgusting, they were all moist and I didn't want to think about what had made them wet. I tried to dry my hands, then I opened the door with the paper towel.

I walked out into the shop. It was always noisy, so no one had heard me bust the mirror. I called out to no one, "Hey, that mirror in the bathroom broke."

Sammy was the closest thing I had to a friend at Gimme A Brake. He said, "What'd you do to it?"

"I didn't do anything to it. It was broken when I went in there." I figured that should be enough to cover my ass. I looked around the shop. It was a specialty brake shop that had the City's demographics. I didn't look like anybody in the place. Sammy was a white guy, about my age. John, the shop owner was a stocky

Chinese guy in his fifties. Jerry was an African American guy around fifty who had zero sense of humor. There was a Latino in his thirties and a white guy in his forties. I didn't know anything about any of them. Then there was me. And what the fuck was I? That's what I thought when I looked in the mirror. I was white, but I didn't realize I was white till I was twenty-two. I grew up in the Mission and was surrounded by Latinos and one day I looked in the mirror and thought, "Oh my god, I'm white." I was white. It was a shock. I was white and plain. I looked more boy than girl, and was average build, but shorter than the average human, just over five feet tall and people always thought I was a junior high school boy. I was short, and my lack of stature reflected my importance in the world: small. Small and disposable. I don't know what was going on, but there was no way for me to feel comfortable or at peace in this body in my adventure on Planet Earth.

So, I always felt out of place. So what. Right at that moment I was a drudge working in a brake shop and I needed to look busy. Everyone had figured out I didn't know shit about brake jobs and that I had lied my way into this place because I was desperate for money. I walked past Jerry, he was working on a blue Corolla, I think he was bleeding the brakes. I went over to his Snap-On toolbox. The Snap-Ons are very cool, fire engine red and really heavy. I was not much taller than the toolbox. I ran my fingers down the toolbox drawers, selected one, yanked the handle, and I accidentally pulled the drawer all the way out. I didn't think they came all the way out, but every damn wrench, screwdriver and socket in that drawer fell to the ground. Jerry stood next to the Corolla and watched as every single metal object fell and clanged on the concrete floor. You should have seen his face. He was pissed! It was an accident.

Jerry came over to me and I thought he was gonna hit me. "Whaddya doin', jackass?" he yelled.

I grabbed a wrench from the floor and ran over to the passenger side rear brakes, tightening the bolt that held the brake pad. I was really trying to do my best, so I pulled it tighter and tighter, when all of a sudden, I really don't know what it was, the bolt snapped or something, and both the wrench and the brake pad flew. "Uh oh," I said.

Jerry said, "You broke it! Stupid dyke!"

That was it. The bolt had snapped, then Jerry snapped, and then I snapped. That was all he needed to say to me. It was one thing if I used that word, but others don't get that privilege. I clenched my hands, my shoulders rose like a dog's hackles, and I charged at him. "What'd you call me?" I picked up a big wrench and threw it full force at Jerry. Jerry ducked and the wrench hit the Corolla windshield. The wrench landed on the bucket seat, and the windshield safety glass crumbled into a billion mini ice cubes. The other guys in the shop had circled around to see what was going on. Sammy had a greasy red rag, and he slapped it in his hand—that's about all I remember of the circle.

Jerry looked at me and said, "I called you a stupid dyke!!"

I stood there for half a second then I said, "I'm not stupid!"

That's when John walked over. He looked at the broken windshield, then at Jerry, then at me. John sighed in a way that I knew meant he had reached the end of his rope, called it quits, given up. Again, I don't know why, but I had another wrench in my hand so I swung it at Jerry. John grabbed my arm before I did anything, but it's not like I meant to hurt Jerry. I just wanted to shut him up. Well, that was that. John took the wrench away and marched me into his office.

John's office was a real pit. It looked as if years of motor oil and coffee had absorbed into the walls. And the décor was half male chauvinism and half Chinese culture. There were auto part sponsored posters of bikini clad girls posing on cars, and it looked like they'd been stuck on the wall to absorb the grease slick. There were also a lot of signs, some real, like OSHA standards and some just goofy, like "Don't go away angry, just go away." Then there were lots of Chinese things, like a calligraphy wall hanging, a Chinese bank calendar (hung upside down for luck), some lucky bamboo, a happy cat, a mini brass dragon, and a lucky turtle.

John was all right. I can't really say anything terrible about him. Dammit. He sat behind his desk and stubbed a cigarette out in a dirty ashtray. He was chunky and, like I said, the wrong side of 50. He had been talking, but I hadn't been listening. He glared at me then spoke some more. "I didn't say you NEED to apologize, I said you BETTER apologize."

I looked away. "Okay," I said, "I'm sorry." I took a beat. "I'm sorry he called me stupid." The door was half-open, and I could see Sammy lingering and listening. "Look John, it's like this. They hate me because I'm gay."

John said, "No, they just hate you." He got up from his chair. "Well, this is it." He stood and it looked like he was gonna run out of the room. "You're outta here."

Outta here? I couldn't be outta here. It was the twenty-second day of June. I had begged my roommate, Kim, to cover my rent till the fifteenth. By the way, she didn't. I had promised I'd pay her back on the fifteenth. But Kim wouldn't front me the money, so I hadn't paid rent... again. I couldn't get fired! And I also couldn't tell Kim that I hadn't paid the rent since January. Six months meant eviction and if I got evicted, she got evicted because we were both on the lease. I was going to have to put on an Oscar-worthy performance to convince John to keep me. I needed cash!

"Why? He started it!"

"Why?" said John. "Because you almost clocked the stupid sonofabitch in the head with a wrench!"

"It's not like I hit his soft spot or anything."

"Out," John said.

Apparently, I wasn't going to be taking home the Oscar this year. "All right," I said. "I was tired of working for the man anyway." And I just stood there.

"Do you know what your problem is?" He said it with that sound. You know the sound. It was a tone your parents probably used every single day.

"Something tells me I'm going to find out," I said. "So you think I hate myself. Plain and simple."

"I didn't say that," John said.

"No, it is not plain and simple. I hate myself in a magnificent and complex way."

"I was going to say you don't know anything about working in an auto shop."

"You think if I stopped hating myself my life might get better. I might enjoy things. Enjoy things?" I said and then I thought about it for a second. "Pass." I was never going to enjoy things. Life was just too much of a struggle. It was this daily hunt to try and make enough dough to stay alive. It was the endless worry that there was never going to be enough... never enough money, or food, or safety. I was just trying to hang on. I didn't have any energy to enjoy myself. Plus, if I let down my guard, someone was bound to take advantage. I had an edge, and it worked. One of the few things I had learned from my Dad.

"There's the door," John said with a nod to the door.

I was desperate. "Howzabout some severance pay?"

"Severance pay?" John said. "You've broken a brake caliper, destroyed an air gun, cracked the front window, and now a smashed windshield. Even with your last check, you owe us four hundred bucks."

I took a few steps then stopped. "What about a letter of recommendation?"

John was starting to lose his temper. "You don't know how to install brakes! I don't know how you lied your way in here! You're gonna kill someone!"

I walked down the step from the office and back into the shop floor. I had one last idea. It was a long shot, but hey! "How about a case of Pennzoil?"

John pointed his finger to the exit. "Out!"

I walked out the door and started walking down the street. What would I do? I didn't know. I stood on the street, and it was cold and the sky was filled with June gloom. I was in the Tenderloin. The 'Loin was considered kinda gritty and, yeah, there's crime and prostitution and a lot of homeless people, but there are also some outstanding Viet restaurants there and you can eat cheap. I liked the Tenderloin. You just had to look out for the broken glass, used syringes, and the human beings that had been tossed out on the street. That's when I saw this guy who looked homeless, lying in the gutter.

"Young man, young man!" he said. "You shoot pool? You shoot pool?"

This must have been the fifth time some guy in the gutter had challenged me to shoot pool. I always figured they were hoping to cash in on money or drinks. "No, I don't shoot pool," I lied. Why was I talking to this guy? I had my own problems. I was walking down Larkin Street because I thought it wouldn't be as crowded as Polk, but I went a couple blocks and I ended up stuck in this crowd that I realized was a bunch of people who must have been waiting for a methadone clinic to open.

It was only guys and a bunch of them were high, and this one guy was totally loaded and had a syringe in his hand with his arm in the air, pointing the needle to the sky. He was spinning around in circles in this compressed crowd of maybe thirty people. I got stuck in the middle, and I was trapped. I thought the guy was gonna accidentally jab me with the needle and I spun around and around and around, then the crowd spit me back out onto Larkin.

This was my karma. I lived in this rich, snobby, prissy little City and I ended up in the crappiest places and the lousiest situations. Why couldn't I just land in the lap of some fool with a trust fund? No, instead I was stuck in the blue-collar abyss, stuck with a bunch of other saps, but I was the only one that seemed to get fired every month. I didn't really think I deserved to be fired, but was it my karma? Jerry was the one that called me names. I had just wanted to kick his ass. He needed his ass kicked. That was his karma. This lifetime was about righting the karma for those who had been oppressed and historically underrepresented, specifically me.

I felt like I tried and tried and tried and I never got anywhere. I didn't want much. An apartment. Food. Maybe a girlfriend. I didn't think I wanted much. I was willing to work hard… wait, no I wasn't. There were just some basic human rights I deserved whether I had any employment skills or not. I wished John could have seen my side. And given me a raise. I was going to have to find a new job. What could I do? Where could I look? I was good for nothing and I kept thinking about how my father had said I would end up dying, drunk and in the gutter, and as soon as I had walked out of Gimme A Brake I had seen that guy in the gutter. Was it my destiny to end up sleepy and shitfaced in a muddy gutter? Challenging chumps to a game of 8-ball? Why had my father said that? Did he know something I didn't? Was he willing it to happen? Would he be right? My head was spinning.

That's when I saw the drag queen. She was screaming at someone who I guessed was either her boyfriend or a trick. The drag queen was about 5' 10", was mixed, maybe Latina and black, and she wore this skintight, sunshine yellow dress. The dress was trampy in a good way and so bright I wished I had some shades. She wore matching heels, fishnets, and capped off the look with too much makeup and a black beehive. I got closer and figured out the other guy was the boyfriend, based on the argument. He was a white guy with muscles, and he had to be over six feet. "Get the fuck out!" he yelled. "Get out and stay out! I never want to see you again, you stupid, fucking slut!" I was about to say, "It's okay to say I love you," when the white guy clocked the drag queen. The drag queen's legs flew in the air and it felt like they stayed there for a few seconds before she landed on her ass. "I need my clothes," the queen yelled. "I need my wallet!"

"You ain't getting shit!" the bodybuilder boyfriend yelled, and he slammed the gate shut and disappeared.

You know, I'm a germaphobe, but I wasn't going to leave the drag queen flat on her ass. I helped her up, which was a challenge, because she was taller than me and her heels kept slipping. She was crying and her mascara was rolling down her face. She was trying to talk but couldn't get the words out. While I was helping her, I saw bruises on her arms and legs, some new, some old. The boyfriend must have been beating the shit out of her for a long time. After slipping and sliding for a minute, I was able to help prop her up and I was about to go.

"Can you, can you give me some money for the bus? I have to get out of here!!!" she wailed. The sound of her voice. There is nothing like the cry of an abused drag queen. But I needed every dime I had.

I was going to need money for the bus… I was going to need money to get to an interview… I had promised Kim I would buy my own coffee this time. I only had two bucks on me. "I'm lucky he didn't kill me!" the drag queen said. Yes, you are, I thought. Boy, my life was shitty, but it wasn't abused drag queen on the sidewalk shitty. I reached into the pocket of my jeans. I took out the two dollars and looked at them. They were all crumpled up and one of the George Washington's had that smug look on his face that said, "You stupid bitch." I put the two dollars into the drag queen's hand.

"Oh, bless you!" she said. "You are going to have such good karma! Thank you!" Man, she was a wreck, with the snail trails of mascara and the bruises, and I saw that she was missing a tooth.

I kind of shrugged and walked on. I decided to cut over on Turk. I was heading for Café Fleur. I had told Kim I'd meet her for a cup of coffee and maybe the walk would give me enough time to think up a good story about the rent money.

Chapter 2 – Where's the Money, Honey

I had never really had a problem stringing Kim along for the rent money. I don't know why I had a funky feeling that day, as I walked toward Market Street. It would be easy. I'd explain that everyone at the shop was homophobic. Yeah, that sounded good. They all messed with me. They were all out to get me. That's why I got fired. No, I really didn't want to use the word fired. How about this: the owner had an emergency and couldn't pay us for a few weeks, but I would get paid. It would just take a few weeks. What kind of emergency? His wife needed surgery. A hysterectomy. That would work. No one would want any information about that. This whole story was shaping up well. I had a decent feeling this line would work.

It was June. The last time I had paid rent was

December, but Kim didn't know that. She only knew about June. In San Francisco you could be evicted after four months of no rent. I think. I really didn't know the rules. I knew there were a few places to get legal advice, but that's all I knew. I didn't even know what they were called. I had never been this far behind on my rent before. A month, yes. Two months, sure. But six months? Even I would evict myself for that. I didn't know how much longer I could get away with it before a big boot kicked me in the fanny and out the door.

I hit Market Street, near Laguna. It was June and the street was awash with gay flags. I mean more awash than usual. Father's Day had just passed, and the next Sunday would be the Pride Parade. The City was always crazy during Pride Week. Nearly a million people flooded in and they had money and they wanted to party. And this year, 2004, was going to be crazier than ever. In February, Gavin had made gay marriage legal and for a few weeks, gays could get married at City Hall. Gays flooded in and while the social justice was terrific, what was really great was that they bought things. They bought wedding clothes and flowers and hotel rooms and all the silly, expensive things that go with a wedding. That was when I was working at Let Them Eat Cake, a ritzy little cake shop, and we made sixty gay wedding cakes in one month. I got canned from that job because I refused to take an order for a straight couple's wedding cake on religious grounds. It was supposed to be a joke, but Josie, the owner didn't think it was very funny and fired me as soon as she found out about it. After that, I crossed baking off the list. Well gay marriage was legal, then it wasn't legal, then maybe it was again, and that day in June, I wasn't sure if it was or wasn't, but it was going to be a big theme in the Pride Parade. If I had a buck by then I might go; it was always a good time.

But right that second, I wasn't up for a good time. I mean, I was 38 years old, I didn't have a career, and now I didn't even have a job. I was scraping from month to month and my apartment was hanging in the balance. I was two years shy of having a mid-life crisis, and instead all I had was a perpetual crisis. The Universe seemed hell-bent on kicking my ass, but what the Universe didn't seem to get through its thick head was that I always fight back. Life sucked.

If I just had some money, a stash of cash, a small safe, or a job that paid more than minimum wage, life might be worth living. But the daily hell of hoping for a cup of coffee and a hot dog was really getting to me. I was almost middle-aged, and I didn't know what I wanted to do. I didn't have any skills, I didn't have any decent work clothes, and I had 6 college credits in administrative justice. I had once thought I would be a cop until I realized it was much more likely that I would be arrested.

I had arrived at Café Fleur. They had a rod iron fence around the place, with vines growing on the fence, so I guess that was the Fleur. If you enjoy mediocre, overpriced food, condescending, patronizing servers, and the world's most uncomfortable chairs, Café Fleur was the place for you. I liked the place, though the male servers treated the female customers like crap. And I went there almost every day, so they all knew me and yet they treated me like garbage. Just because of the double-X chromosome thing. Café Fleur de Lis was on Market at Noe and you could sit inside or out. I liked sitting outside. Notice I didn't say I liked sitting outside if the weather was good. If I said I like sitting outside when the weather was good, that would mean I'd only sit outside three days a year. It was pretty chilly this June day, but I knew we would be sitting outside. It was nice to sit in the outdoor section where you could watch the boys stroll by, or even better, select a street side seat to pose and be seen.

Though the name of the place was Café Fleur De Lis everyone called the place Café Fleur, or just Fleur. There was a front door if you knew where to look for it. The door was always open so you rarely saw the name was painted on a metal plaque that hung on the rod iron. The painter had crafted an ornate name plate and had painted Café Fleur de Lie on it, not Fleur de Lis. And it WAS Fleur de Lie because the place was crammed with poseurs, now more than ever since the City was already getting overcrowded with Pride Parade visitors. Okay, there were always more poseurs posing on the balcony of the Outlook bar across the street, where bare-chested men would flaunt their six-packs while drinking one, but Fleur ran a close second.

Kim came walking up. She saw me and gave a single wave of her hand. Kim was Filipino, Pinay, born and raised in Daly City. There are so many beautiful Pinays, petite, with long, flowing black hair and a soft, little giggle. Kim wasn't one of them. Kim was about 5' 7", and, I don't mean this in a bad way, but she was pretty damn fat. She wore a severe butch haircut that was shaved all up in the back and the rest of her hair was about a quarter inch long. And man, if I dragged my human form around, Kim lumbered. She always looked tired, like the weight of world was squatting on her Buddy Holly glasses. She wore those checkered chef pants, because she was in culinary school and it was the required uniform. She had her white chef school jacket on, unsnapped, and flipped on her shoulder. Underneath she wore a white wifebeater.

"Hey, why don't you grab a table and I'll get us

some lattes," I said.

"Okay," Kim said.

I touched my pocket. "Oh. I left my cash at home. Gimme a twenty and I'll pay you back."

Kim looked like she was chewing gum, but she didn't have any gum in her mouth. She had a harsh look, what they call today "resting bitch face," but she always had that look on her face. She let out a deadly sigh then pulled a twenty out of her pocket and gave it to me. She went to look for a table. I grabbed the lattes and headed to Kim, and then it happened again. I did one of those things, one of those things that makes no sense, like breaking the mirror, or swinging the wrench.

I saw these two women and they were making out, sharing the tongue. It really made me sick. Not because they were two women, of course, it was the public exchange of bodily fluids. That, plus I just hate seeing anyone happy. I walked up behind them and I pretended to be distracted, looking off to Market Street and I did the ole fake trip and dumped the latte on the top of the head of one of the two lovebirds.

One of them screamed, "What the hell are you doing?"

"Oops. My bad," I said. My bad was such a hella stupid phrase. You weren't sorry. You didn't care. It was a stupid thing to say, but it was a very popular phrase at the time.

"You jackass!" one of the women said. She stood up and told her girlfriend, "Let's get out of here!" They were pissed and left.

I placed Kim's coffee in front of her. Kim was shaking her head. I saw some big-assed server bent over, wiping down the tables. "Hey, garcon! Dude! My latte exploded! The clowns inside must have put the lid on wrong. Another, please. Soy, not milk. A triple soy latte."

Then the server turned around and it was a she, not a he. It was an African American woman, maybe 5' 5", with an average build except for that big round rump. I'd never seen a female server in Café Fleur before but before I could think more, Kim was talking at me.

She said, "You are so very much a jerk."

I held my hands up with a shrug. "What?"

Kim tapped her coffee cup. "Why did you do that?"

I looked at her like I didn't know what she was talking about. "Do what?"

Kim and I had been roommates for a long time.

She didn't need to say a thing. She gave me a look that said, "You know what I mean."

"It was an accident," I said. "My foot got caught on the… thingamajig!"

Kim was sucking her lips in; that was about third degree pissed for her. "You didn't trip," she said.

"Yeah, I tripped!"

"Bullshit."

"Accident! The lid blew off the cup."

"The lid was still on the cup," Kim said. She pointed in the direction of the two women who had left. "See that? That's what people who like themselves look like."

"Oh, the delusions of the masses," I said.

Kim finally took a sip from her coffee. "You're just jealous."

I said, "Jealous? Of that? I don't think so."

Kim said, "You need to get a girlfriend. Then maybe you wouldn't be such an asshole. Why don't you ask that girl at the health food store?"

"They said I couldn't go back in there. Besides, I got a better idea! Why don't I get a new job?"

The look on Kim's face. The sound of her voice.

"Oh gawd, you didn't get fired again, did ya?"

"I need Gimme A Brake like I need a second asshole," I said.

I could see the wheels turning in Kim's head. "Rent's due," she said. "Correction. Rent's late."

"I'll have my money. Plus, they still owe me my last check."

"I can't loan you any more money."

"I said I'd get the money," I said.

"Don't put the place in jeopardy. I can't afford to lose that flat. If I had to find a new place, it'll kill me. And so would a raise in the rent."

"We won't get kicked out," I said.

"I won't get kicked out," Kim said "You better get a job, or you'll be out on your ass. Sleepin' on the sidewalk in the cold San Francisco summer. They'll find your frozen corpse on Gough, a brown-haired popsicle in a grungy sleeping bag."

"Don't make it sound so appealing," I said. I tried to remember my planned speech. "This is all Gimme A Brake's fault. They don't value women. They hate gays… oh, no, wait. The boss, his wife needed surgery and he needed every dime he has, and he had to hold our checks."

Kim rolled her eyes up to the sky and shook her head. "You are a really shitty friend, you know that? And if you're gonna constantly be a shitty friend, you should at least learn how to lie better."

"Lie? Me?" and I touched my heart to show how fucking sincere I was. That's when the cute server returned and brought me a new latte. She kind of slammed it in front of me. "Thanks," I said and I tried to smile and look hella cheerful, and even I knew it was frightening. The server kind of jerked back in reaction, like she was startled, and she immediately left. I looked at Kim. "I even scare myself." I waited and Kim said nothing. "You're supposed to say it's not that bad."

Kim looked at me. "Uh…. Yeah."

"And I'm not a liar," I said.

"Oh please." She tried to mimic my voice, "The stove was already broken! I didn't kick that cat! I took the trash out; they must have skipped us! Maybe aliens drank the rest of the Cabernet. I didn't give that boss a heart attack!"

It was really lame to have to listen to my own crap and to realize that Kim knew I was permanently full of shit. The black woman was wiping off the table where I had dumped the latte. She was somewhere in her 30s I guessed, and she wore a short, cropped 'fro. Each time the woman wiped the table she was shoving that ass right up to my face. I finally whispered to Kim. "Damn! That ass! Those slacks are about to explode!" and I made an explosion sound. With every scrub, she just kept pumping that butt into my face. Right when I couldn't take it anymore, she leaned totally across the table and shoved her big, solid rump into our table. She finally finished and left. I grabbed some napkins and mopped my brow. "Whew!" I fanned myself with a napkin. "That ass!"

"Why don't you ask her out?" Kim asked.

"Why?" I said. "We'd only break up in a week."

"Yeah, but it would give the rest of us five days of peace."

"Aah, there's no way she'd like me. I mean, she's an upwardly mobile coffee girl... and I'm a downwardly plunging unemployed loser. I'll just skip to the part where we already broke up and I'll just be angry at her. Who needs her anyway? Besides, I already have a job interview tomorrow."

"Think you'll get it?" Kim asked

"I better."

"You bet you better. Three weeks late on your rent."

"I'm totally qualified," I said.

"Why don't ya tell 'em why you got fired from the last job?" Kim said.

"I'll skip that part," I said.

"Well… I hope you get it."

"Nothing's worked out for me so far. And I'm almost forty! The Universe just likes screwing me. I'm sure it'll want me to continue grabbing my ankles."

"I dunno. Why don't you ask the Universe for a change?"

I pressed my palms together and looked skyward. "Universe, pretty please, may I fuck you in the ass for a change? Instead of me always getting it rammed up mine? Hey, what about you?"

Kim drained the last of her coffee. "I don't like it up the ass."

"So I've heard," I said. "But what I meant was money. If you could give me a month – "

"Sorry, I'm tapped."

"What about your parents?"

"Right." The sarcasm flooded the air like the smell of a burnt panini. "I'm gonna ask my elderly parents, on a fixed income, to loan you money? The parents who stopped talking to me the day I came out. The parents who haven't seen me for years?"

"They probably have some savings." I pointed out.

"You are so fucked up."

"I'm trying to change."

"Look. I've been meaning to talk to you about this anyway. Brenda wants to move in. Correction, I want Brenda to move in. If you can't make rent this month, maybe it's time for you to start looking for a new place."

"Kim, we're roommates," I said.

"Yeah. Things change," she said.

"But this can't change. Not right now. I mean. I've got to…. I can't find a new place to live right now. And I have no place to go."

"I can't pay your way anymore," Kim said.

This was a bit of an unexpected bombshell. And not Brenda. She was such a non-entity. I was a great roommate, I mean at least there was always something going on, a story to keep the roomie amused, a little drama to make the world go 'round. But I couldn't get kicked out. And what if Kim found out I was behind not one month. Six months. Two months past eviction. The only way she'd be able to stay would be to pay all my back rent and there was no way she could do it. There had to be a way out of this, but for the moment, I didn't know what it was. I was holding my breath.

"Really, all you need is a little confidence," Kim said.

"Nah, I don't need that," I said. "I need cash. Maybe I should go to bartending school."

"That's your solution to everything. Bartending school. You don't want to be a bartender."

"It would pay the bills," I said.

"Bartending school costs money. You have no money. No money means no bartending school."

"Man, no bartending school. And I could really use a drink right now."

We both sat there for a couple of minutes, the mustard gas of "MOVE OUT" still lingering in the air between us. Finally, Kim said she was going to class and I said I'd walk with her.

Chapter 3 – Funny Money

You know that geometry thing that says the shortest distance from Point A to Point B is a straight line? Kim Macadangdang must have never taken geometry because she never went directly anywhere. I get it. Nobody in the Castro wanted to do anything straight, but she would meander in odd directions, or through back streets, ignoring the fastest route. It made me crazy. I think she was always avoiding going wherever she needed to go. So we walked up Noe through the Duboce Triangle. The Duboce Triangle is north of Castro and it's relatively safe. The biggest danger is you might slip on some dog shit, which is everywhere since there were more dogs than kids in San Francisco, and there were tons of dog owners who left their dog dingle littered on the sidewalks.

"Did you tell Lynne?" Kim asked.

"Tell her what?" Like I didn't know.

"Tell her that you don't have the rent. You need to tell her as soon as you get home. I can't lose that place."

"Stupid landlords," I said. "You know, everything and everyone on this planet is out to get me. And I have to punch and kick and bite just to survive."

"You think you're fighting the world, but you're really just fighting yourself."

"Well the good thing about fighting myself is I always win!"

"And you always lose, too," Kim said.

We walked up Hermann. The slow-ass J Train was riding up Church like a slug with a death rattle. "Of course that damn train comes when I don't need it," I said.

"You gotta do something. Get your shit together."

"I don't even know why I try. I'll ask Chad. Maybe he can loan me some cash. Though it makes no difference. Sooner or later, I'll end up here." I pointed my thumb at the cement fortress on our right. "At our local prison."

Kim looked at the building, then at me. "That's the U.S. Mint, dumbass."

"So glad we have a national breath freshener. What's our state chewing gum?"

"It's the Mint!" Kim yelled. "The United States Mint! They make money there. You know – the Mint!"

"Do you mean The Mint bar?" It was a few blocks away and, by the way, their karaoke is legendary.

"It's the Mint!"

"I thought the Mint was that public urinal on 5th."

"That's the Old Mint," Kim said. "This is the New Mint."

"Wow. There so much construction going on in the City. I guess I didn't notice 'em put it up."

Kim got frustrated a lot. And for no reason. "It was built in the thirties!" she yelled.

"The 1930's? News flash, sistah. It ain't that new."

I looked at the Mint. There was a reason I had thought it was a prison. It was four giant slabs of gray. It sat on a rocky hill above Market Street and to say it was imposing would be an understatement.

It looked like an angry box made of fog. Maybe the world's least happy birthday cake. River rocks decorated the base and the rest was cold concrete. If a dyspeptic drill sergeant could be a building, this was it.

It was like someone had taken the Alcatraz prison and plopped it on the hill above Safeway. Correction, the prison at Alcatraz seemed more homey than this joint. It was very plain and very strict, just walls of gray with tall windows. I mean two- or three-story high windows, unusually tall, skinny windows. They stretched into oversized rectangles with either a shade, or maybe it was just a reflection, I wasn't sure. I counted the windows (something I learned from being caught in a riot – get counts), thirteen tall windows, then another window on each side that didn't exactly match. Then there were tiny, little square windows above them, thirteen of those. And there were windows below the tall ones, and all of them had bars on them. This dive looked like it had been built from gray, concrete bricks. Up at the top, there were circular plaques between each window. There was some lettering, but I couldn't make it out and couldn't see what the plaques were either. An American flag flapped up top, in the center. Like I said, the base was rock, real rock, and steps led up to an entry gate. The whole place was fenced, and there was barbed wire, not your basic barbed wire, and not your run of the mill concertina wire, no, they had razor wire. They meant business.

I guessed there might be a parking lot in the back, but I wasn't sure. To the side of the entrance were metal turnstile doors, like at the zoo, the ones that don't let you sneak back in. To the right of the turnstile was an intercom, and a few steps up from the door was the station for security guards. It didn't look like it would be easy to get in or out of this fortress.

"They make money there," Kim said.

"They make money there?" I asked.

"Yeah."

"Funny money," I said.

"Not funny money. Real money. They have to print money somewhere. Haven't you ever seen those giant sheets of bills?"

I had seen those giant sheets of bills, portrait after portrait of Ben Franklin, just waiting to be cut into cold, hard cheddar. I hadn't really thought about where they actually printed up money. But here it was, right in my backyard, the cash cow, the money tree, the goose that laid the golden egg, and it had been sitting there, blocks away from me, all this time.

"At least somebody's makin' money," Kim said.

"Yeah. It should be that easy. All these years I been bustin' my hump for minimum wage when I coulda just busted into this place to STEAL minimum wage!"

"Right," Kim said. "Look at it. That place is a fortress. And you can barely get a candy bar out of a vending machine. You have no skills."

"I do have one skill. I can pick locks. My deranged daddy taught me before he decided he wanted to set up house in San Quentin." I looked at those gray cement blocks. "I could just pick a lock. Load up a backpack of freshly minted moola and kick back for the rest of my life."

"You can't pick a lock. You couldn't even open your own combo lock at the pool. Anyway. You're outta your freakin' mind. Look at it. It's thirty feet of cement. You can't just 'pick a lock.' See that?" She pointed at the building. "That's a video camera. And look. They're everywhere. And a security station. That means guards. And it's a federal building." We both looked down the line at camera after camera after camera. "You can't break into that big slab of concrete, fuckin' doofus."

"Let's look on the other side," I said.

"Sure," Kim said. "They reinforced this side but

left the other side open for anyone who wants to break in. Forget it. You're a fucking idiot. You're not robbing the Mint, and I can't be late for class."

"I could just sneak in there and pull fresh sheets of cash right off the presses and all my problems would be solved."

"Yeah," said Kim. "And I could just pull a white rabbit out of my ass."

"Oh, I'd like to see that!" I said. Kim may have thought I was a shitty friend, but bottom line, we were friends. We enjoyed each other's company and it helped ease the daily suffering.

Kim's class was on Polk and we ended up at City Hall, so I told Kim we should walk through it. It was still open, and we walked up the steps on the Van Ness side. I extended my arm, letting Kim go first through the revolving doors. As soon as she revolved, I hit the door hard, launching her out. She rolled her eyes. We both went through the metal detectors then landed on the main floor.

"I dunno why they use those metal detectors. There hasn't been a mayor worth shooting in decades," I said.

"What about Di-Fi?"

"She wasn't even worth taking the safety off.

And Willie Brown. He was such a damn playa no one would want to take him out. He was enjoyable."

"What about Agnos?"

"He got shot. Not at City Hall. The Zebra Killer, but still."

"Frank Jordan?"

"Oh gawd, no."

"What about Gavin Newsom?"

"Nah, we gotta protect Newsom. For starters, I think he plays for our team. And I wish I "Knew Some" of his boyfriends, so I could prove it." We walked out the doors onto the Polk Street side.

Kim pointed back at City Hall. "Why'd you make me do that?"

"Do what?"

"Walk through City Hall. The metal detectors are a pain in the ass." This from the person who could not take a shortcut.

"Excuse me, my taxes pay for that place. I like to think it's my vacation home. And look, I own all this!" I held my arms out to the Civic Center Plaza. The Plaza was an aesthetic nightmare. Boring strips of lawn and cement, two small children's playgrounds where kids could ride swings, play tag, or play hide 'n' go seek for syringes in the sand. Several homeless people slept in the grass, and a few drank from brown bags; no judgment here—it could have been iced tea. There was a group of people doing Tai Chi and they were trying to intimidate the people doing Falun Gong. To the north, there was a strange, enclosed strip of elevators that went to the parking garage. An oblong coffee stand was parked inside the glass cube that housed the elevators. A hot dog cart was near the curb.

But the weirdest thing in Civic Center Plaza was these two rows of flags. About fifty feet separated the rows of flags that flanked the walk to City Hall. Each side had nine flagpoles, with about ten feet between the poles. The line also has the world's oddest trees, all mangled and deadheaded.

I stood on the sidewalk, held my arms out, and yelled, "It's a world of freaks and I'm a loyal citizen!"

We walked down the City Hall steps. I dodged cars, crossed the street, and walked through the plaza. A protester came up, gave me a flyer, and said, "Falun Gong is not a crime."

"I know," I said. As much as most of the world annoyed me, I was for everything. And I especially had no issue with Falun Gong, since I was clueless about it.

It didn't look political – it looked like Tai Chi.

"Going through the metal detectors wastes five minutes."

My mind was somewhere else, and I said, "Life's just not fair."

"Well, it is only five minutes," Kim said.

"I don't mean the metal detectors," I said. "I mean in general. Life's not fair."

"No one said it would be."

"I did, ya Filipina Bozo!"

"Dumbass Cracker!"

"Starfleet Academy Dropout!"

"Flow-bee Using Tool!"

"Karaoke Has-Been!"

"Gay Softball League Reject!"

"Ow. That one hurts. There's only one place left to go."

"Don't go there," Kim said.

"You! You, the great chef du jour. You drink wine from a box!"

"Ooh. Man, you play dirty… and if you ever tell

anyone that I ever drank wine from a box, you will pay for the rest of your life! Anyway, I'm outta ammo. We'll pick this up later."

"Okay," I said. Some friends gave hugs. Some friends shared supportive words. For Kim and I, we shared insults. This is how we knew we were friends, messy rent situation and all. We kept walking through Civic Center, but Kim was walking farther away from where she was going.

"Class is that-a-way," I pointed in the opposite direction.

"I don't want to be late, but I don't want to go. Stupid California Culinary College. Every frikken jerk there treats me like a second-class citizen! I don't know why. And my student loans have piled up like the debt of a third world country. My whole life I dreamed of going there! Now I'm there and I hate it!"

"So you hate it," I said. "At least you have a dream."

"More like a fucking nightmare."

"I wish I had a dream to hate."

"It makes me sick to my stomach!" Kim said.

"Maybe it's salmonella. Or E. coli."

"I started out making pizzas. I wanted my own restaurant! Now I'll be lucky to get any job anywhere so I can pay off my student loans! And I'm still working at the same pizza parlor! I'll be stuck making pizza the rest of my life!"

"That reminds me. Can ya bring home some leftovers tonight?"

"It doesn't work like that!"

"Anything, I'm not picky. But preferably some prime rib. Not so rare this time. I wanna eat it, not notify its next of kin." That's when this homeless guy grabbed my pants leg. I tried to dodge him, but he grabbed me. He was probably in his 70s, dirty, and out of it.

"Son," he said. "Son! Young man!"

I pulled my pants leg away from him. As a card-carrying germaphobe I just don't want anyone touching me. "Yeah?" I said.

"Got a quarter?

"No, I don't got a quarter."

"Ahright, ahright," he said. "Got a dollar?"

"No, old dude, I don't got no dollar either. I don't got no money for your hooch fund, your hoochie fund, or your sushi fund. Dang! The frikken'

Universe must think I'm made out of spare change. I'd like to help you out, but I don't have any money!"

"Ahright, ahright. Remember." The old guy held his finger in the air to make his point. "Always be what you is. Cause if you ain't what you is, then you is what you ain't."

"Terrific idea, Pops," I said, and he sort of collapsed back down. I didn't know if he was drunk or having an episode, but it was just one more example of why we need services. Kim needed to be heading up to the Culinary College, but she just kept walking around Civic Center. I followed. But I couldn't just saunter along. I needed to vent. Constantly.

"Dang," I said, "I never thought my life would turn out this way!"

Kim said, "You mean that you'd be gay?"

"Nah, I always knew that. I meant that life would suck so royally. Well, no job, no flat, no future. I guess this is it. I'm gonna kill myself."

"Oh gawd. Here we go again."

"Yeah, I'll be gone, and everyone'll be sorry."

"No one will be sorry," Kim said.

"When I've croaked, I won't need a job."

"You're not doing shit."

"Yeah," I said. "Cash in my chips. End it all. Universe! Should I continue or call it quits? If only there was a sign! Universe! Should I forge on, or bow out gracefully, or maybe not so gracefully? Universe, I need a sign, dang it!"

That's when Kim pointed to one of the flags in the Civic Center. I had never really noticed them before, and I looked this one up since. It's called the Commodore Perry flag. This one was a dark blue flag with large white print that read: DON'T GIVE UP THE SHIP.

"There's your answer," Kim said.

"Excuse me, I said a sign, not a flag." I couldn't believe it. I had asked for a response and the universe replied. I hadn't expected an answer, especially not such a specific one. "That is the stoooooopidest thing I've ever seen!"

"No, it's the stoooooopidest SIGN you've ever seen."

"Dang!" I said. "Don't Give Up The Ship. Now I have to continue my odyssey on Planet Earth!"

"I've never noticed those before," Kim said. She pointed at a flag that had a funny shaped tree on it. "That one must be go green."

I found a plaque. "It's the Massachusetts Navy Pine Tree flag."

"Why no gay flag?"

I kept reading the plaque. "They're from the Revolutionary War!"

"Oh, that's why no gay flag," Kim said. "They weren't fighting for our freedom. And they didn't have a flag for oppressing us."

"Sure they did," I said. "The stars and stripes."

"Well, at least you got a sign."

"Gads. Continue! That means I have to make a living. Or maybe it's a sign to follow my folly and rob the U.S. Mint."

"You ain't robbin' shit."

"You need cash as much as I do. You can rob the Mint with me. What about the loans? You said that chef's school's not cheap."

"I'll pay 'em off after I'm out," Kim said.

"How much do you owe?" I asked. Kim hesitated then whispered in my ear. "Holy shit-take mushrooms! That's ten times what I thought. You'll be in debt the rest of your life."

Kim was bothered and looked at the ground. "So,

I'm in debt. It's better than jail."

"That kind of debt is jail!"

"Stealing's not my thing, okay? Maybe you should try and get a City job. Anyway, you know the deal. Get the rent or Brenda's moving in on the first."

She hadn't forgotten or ignored the rent. She brought it up again. That had never happened before. Gawd, don't let her find out about the other months. "Lookit. Thirty minutes. Maybe twenty-seven. At the Mint. We could get sheets and sheets of hundred-dollar bills. There's probably like twenty hundreds on a sheet. That's two grand a sheet! You could pay off your loans and open your own restaurant. You'd be free to do whatever you wanted."

"It's a frikken' felony!" Kim said.

"Wouldn't it be great to shake your fist behind someone's back and yell, 'I showed you! I showed you!' Wouldn't it?"

"I'm not all vengeful like that."

"You could open one of those high-end restaurants. With the glass mosaic splash back and stuff. And the black leather booths."

Kim said, "Those black leather booths cost a small fortune."

"Have you seen those uncut sheets of money?"

"Yes, I brought it up to you."

"One sheet of Ben Franklins must be five grand! Twenty of those and you've got your restaurant. Man! We could both walk out with over a million bucks. An easy million, tucked into your back pocket."

"It's a pipe dream, jackass, and the only question is what are you smokin' in it? Weed or crack?"

"Man, I'm almost forty and I got nothin'! I don't want to worry about rent. And I want… things! You know. Stuff. I'm not all into material possessions… but I'd like some material possessions!"

"You're an idiot."

"You're awfully pissy today."

Kim looked away. "They announce the internships tonight." I'd totally forgotten. This was the culmination of the class, and the best students got the best placement. If you were good, the restaurant usually hired you. Kim was counting on a good placement. "I better get the Quince!" she said. "Or The Boulevard. Or at the very least, Postrio. I'm one of the best chefs in my class and if I can get hired, then I can start paying off the loans. Listen to me. Hard work pays off. Don't jeopardize your future by doing something stupid."

"Stupid might just pay off."

"Stupid never pays off. You gotta get a job. It's only a month's rent. So, what are you gonna do?"

"I dunno," I said. "Anything but fast food."

"Look at that one," Kim said and pointed to a flag. Turns out it was the "Don't Tread on Me" flag, but the wind had blown, and a fold hid the "T" in "Tread."

"Don't read on me? I don't get it. But I get that!" I said and I pointed to the flag that read "Live Free or Die." "Live Free or Die. Wish I was free to do or say or think whatever I want."

"You've always said or done whatever you want."

"Yeah, but I didn't enjoy it. Live free or die."

"Guess that leaves you only one option," Kim said and then she did her best Bette Davis impersonation. "Ya gonna die, Blanche, ya gonna die!"

That was all I needed to hear as I left her at the Culinary College and headed home. Lynne would be there, and she'd want the rent. Would she evict me? Or, rather, would she evict us?

Chapter 4 – Landlord

I stood in front of the door to Lynne's flat. Kim and I lived in the bottom flat, Lynne lived in the center flat, and Chad lived in the top unit. I knocked as softly as I could. There was no answer. I was safe! No one home. I had done what I told Kim I would do and there were no immediate consequences. I turned and had taken a step when Lynne opened the door.

Lynne was in her fifties. She was straight, well as far as I knew she was straight. She was large and dressed in an earth mama style, wearing these soft paisley dresses and stuff. Her hair was always styled, and she wore a lot of makeup and jewelry. Her place was nice. She had a lot of money; her grandma had died or something and left her enough for a down payment on the building and Lynne had enough left over to buy real furniture. There was a cushy couch with throw pillows and a coffee table and even a matching chair. There were really colorful, vibrant fabrics that had been carefully placed around the flat, and light streamed in through the large living room window. The built-ins shelved a lot of self-help books and chochkies, stuff like a drum and a goddess sculpture, a lot of new age things. The flat felt homey and safe. Like half of San Francisco, Lynne was an MFCC and you couldn't open your mouth without getting analyzed and getting a bunch of advice on how to be better.

I stood in the door frame wondering what to say. "Um…."

Lynne raised an eyebrow, then said, "Kim already told me."

"Great!" I said. I wasn't going to have to say anything.

"Not so great," Lynne said. "I need the rent. That's how I pay the mortgage." She grabbed me by the jacket and pulled me into the flat. She sat on the couch while I stood nearby to plead my case.

"Just gimme a month or two and I'll be rollin' in dough. If you could just front me till then…." Wow. I was really embarrassed at the sound of my voice – it reeked of desperation.

"Why don't you break down and ask your Dad if

he can give you some money?"

"Cause he's a drunk," I said. "And I'd guess he's invested his life savings in a suitcase of Budweiser. Plus, since I haven't spoken to him in twenty years, asking for money is probably not the best way to break the ice." Maybe it was more like ten years since I had talked to him, but whatever. He had gone to prison and got out and I really didn't even know where he was.

"Kim said you got fired. How many jobs have you had this year?"

"Three," I said.

"Five," Lynne said.

"That's still less than one per month," I said, looking on the bright side. "Anyway, I'll pull it together. It's only a month's rent."

"No, it's six months' rent. You haven't paid in six months."

"Let me just concentrate on this one month!" Again, the horrid sound of a desperate soul.

"Six months is eviction."

"C'mon, Lynne! You can't kick me out!"

Lynne took a curl of her light brown hair and

pushed it behind her ear. "I'd have to evict both of you. You have a lease."

"You can't kick Kim out! She's paid!"

Lynne shifted on the couch and pulled one leg up, bending her knee. "The rent, in full, hasn't been paid for six months." There was a pause, then she said, "I have a cousin who'd like to move in."

"Oh, so it's like that. You wanna move in a relative for a year so you can buy them out then raise the rent to whatever you want," I said. Everybody in San Francisco did this. This was not good. Lynne had a plan.

Lynne's comfy little pose on the couch was gone in an instant and she sat straight up. "I'd only raise it to market value! I'm barely making it!"

"I knew it!" I said. "I KNEW you were a slumlord! You just want to jack up the rent!"

"If I was a slumlord, I would have already kicked you out." There was a silence for a bit, then Lynne added, "You're the one who hasn't paid."

"Look, if I lose this place, I can't afford another apartment in the City! And if I have to leave the City, I'll die. They'll kill me in a hot minute!"

Lynne sighed and her exhale was just full of

judgment. Like how parents sigh. Like they know everything. "Things aren't like that anymore."

"They are! They are like that. And what about Kim?"

"It's not like it's news to her. She's known you haven't paid."

I tried to keep a poker face, but unfortunately, I have more of a Crazy Eights face.

"Oh, I see," Lynne said. "She DOESN'T know." Lynne played more with her hair and seemed to be trying to calm herself down. Then there was the bombshell that the whole world seemed to want to constantly drop on me. "You know what your problem is?"

"I'm afraid I'm about to find out," I said.

"You hate yourself." It was so simple for other people to sum it up for me. Lynne continued. "When you like yourself, the world likes you back. And when you hate yourself..." Lynne extended her palm toward me wanting me to finish the sentence.

"When you hate yourself, you get the life I've got."

"You're afraid to get close to anyone," Lynne said.

"Yeah, that's because there's a lot of TB in the City."

"You have a classic rejection of your female side."

"I'm glad I stick to the classics," I said.

"You know, Jung described this internal battle between the anima and the animus, this dilemma to unite both male and female Archetypes within ourselves."

I couldn't take anymore. I said, "Gads, if I pay the rent, will you stop?"

"This is what I do all day," Lynne said.

"Annoy people?" I asked.

"Coach them. This rejection of the feminine may be what causes your ongoing self-sabotage. Your life could really change if you'd embrace the feminine."

"Embrace the feminine? Ick. I don't even want to touch it."

Lynne relaxed again on the couch. "There's a lot of power in the feminine."

"Um, yeah," I said. "Why would I want to sit around in a dress, crying all day, when I can kick ass?"

Lynne said, "I don't mean living out your

stereotyped notions of a girl. I mean activating your feminine – your creativity, your empathy, your soul. But since you brought it up, when was the last time you cried, anyway?"

"When I was six."

"You haven't cried since you were six?" Lynne asked. "What happened then? It must have been something big."

I said, "My play-doh dick fell off."

"I'm being serious," Lynne said.

"So am I."

Lynne fluffed up one of the couch pillows. "You need to change," she said.

"I'm almost forty. I'm not going to change!"

"Then let's say find some new coping strategies. Some people turn things around with anti-depressants."

"I don't need Prozac!" I yelled. "I need cash!"

"You've got to break that poverty mentality. You're a prisoner of the way you think. You've got to break the shackles!"

"Thanks, I find my shackles quite comforting. Plus, they're the only bling I have."

"The world is abundant. Start believing that and

you'll see it's for real. You're the one that cuts yourself off from abundance. You know, I used to be a lot like you. As I got older, I mellowed."

"Funny," I said. "I don't see mellow in my near future."

"I can help you all I can. Until I have to – you know – evict you. I'll give you life coaching for free."

"Um. No thanks," I said, though I was thinking about it. Not because I wanted coaching, but because agreeing to it might give me a better opportunity to guilt Lynne into not kicking me out. She must have been thinking the same thing.

"I'm doing it. Then I won't have to feel guilty for kicking you out. I'll know I did everything I can. The coaching can make a big difference. Then maybe you wouldn't be angry night and day."

"I am not angry night and day! Just the day."

"Listen, A.J., I don't mean this in a bad way, but you are the most negative person I know."

"That's because I'm going for the Guinness World Record, stupid bitch." Dammit. As soon as it came out of my mouth, I regretted it. And I could see the little feminine gears cranking away in Lynne's brain.

"Now that I'm your life coach, let me give you your first assignment. Every time you want to say the word 'bitch' I want you to substitute the word 'friend.' Think you can do that?"

I hesitated but I just couldn't resist. "No… friend."

"Trust me. Try it. You'll be much happier."

I felt I had Lynne exactly where I wanted her. "And if I follow your life coaching will I keep the apartment?"

"You've got two weeks," she said. "Get the rent or you and Kim can start shopping for a new place."

"Kim's my best friend," I said, and I left.

It wasn't what I wanted, but it was a two-week reprieve. Maybe I could pull it off… yeah, and maybe I could go straight. Put on a wedding dress and marry some guy and suck his cock for ten minutes a week. This was all possible, but highly unlikely. There was only one way out of this and my conversation with Lynne had settled it. I was gonna rob the U.S. Mint. But I was gonna need some help and I knew exactly where to find it.

Chapter 5 – Oops, I Did it Again

I clomped up the stairs with my soft, dainty little feet. Sometimes you need advice. It's always best to get your advice from someone who will answer with what you want to hear. I needed to see Chad.

The door was always open to Chad's place and before I even got close, I could hear Britney Spears blaring. Chad's place was nice. It was mostly Crate and Barrel, a polished, upscale look with some key items that included this outrageously large glass vase that was usually filled with open blue irises. He had a martini tray with glasses and a shaker on his dining room table – well, let's start there; he had a dining room table, and that was more than most of my friends. That martini shaker looked cool, but I had never seen him use it; it was just for decoration. He had a one-bedroom. All of his stuff seemed nice and new. I don't think he made much money, so I'm not sure how he pulled it off. Chad was 42. I knew that because he always made a big deal about his birthday, which was in August, a Leo, of course. Chad was an attention-seeking rocket.

Chad was cool enough. He was a white guy who was always seeking some kind of ethnic roots. He couldn't just settle into being a decent looking white guy and being happy with that. He was always assuming an additional identity, sort of a flava of the year, Latin or Asian or, his current interest, of culturally appropriating all things African American, well, more or less. Britney Spears wasn't exactly gangsta rap.

As soon as I hit the third floor, I saw Chad in Catholic school drag. A little white blouse and a red, plaid, pleated mini skirt. He was lip-synching to "Oops, I Did it Again." He had fashioned up a little routine with some super slutty choreography. He was sort of humping the dining room chair when he saw me at the door and ran over. He kind of grabbed me, then dropped it down low and popped back up while I watched, uncomfortably. "Dude!" I said. "Britney Spears? Really?"

That's when he kicked his leg up and I saw more than I cared to, so I shielded my eyes. "Oh, commando! No! NO!" I yelled. My resistance fueled him even more. He pulled me into his apartment, turned off the music, and sang.

"Oops, I did it again! I wiggled my ass, in front of my friend!" And as he sang, he showed his ass, right in my face. Definitely cringeworthy.

"Oh yeah, that's nice," I said sarcastically.

Chad stopped with the wiggle. "What's wrong?" He asked. "My ass usually cheers you up."

I slumped down on his fancy couch. "Ah Chad, even your freshly waxed butt cheeks can't hoist me out of my misery today. I'm broke, dude. I need cash. Lynne's gonna toss me in the streets. And Kim too. I wish things worked out, but…."

Chad said, "Work out? I've been working out. Watch this!" Chad tried to do the splits. We can all have desires. Things we want to do, things we wish we can do. But when you're a six-foot man over forty, doing the splits should be crossed off the list. He was on the floor, trying to force his right leg down and it wasn't going to happen. It was painful for him to try, and painful for me to watch. He finally struggled back up.

"…But how do you do it?" I asked.

"Quite simple," Chad said. "I just fold and tuck. It hurts, but it hurts so good! Sometimes a little Vaseline petroleum jelly."

"I meant… oh, forget it." I was gonna explain

that I was asking how he made things work out, but why ask? "Look Chad, I need your help."

"Y-e-a-h," he said, and he really stretched the word out. "You still owe me money."

"I'm not here to borrow money. Although I'd take it if you gave it to me. I need your advice. Just come with me."

Chad wasn't the type of person who asked where or why. He changed into a t-shirt and jeans and before you know it, we had walked up Church Street and stood outside Out of the Closet, a used clothing store. A super-hoochiefied outfit had been strapped on a mannequin and Chad drooled over it.

"Look at it," he said.

"Look at what?" I asked.

"Isn't it beautiful?"

"Hmm," I said. I guess I had a different idea of beauty. I'd say it was slutty.

"If only I owned that ensemble," Chad said, and he said ensemble the French way. "Then I could win Miss Ghetto Fabulous."

"Um, yeah, Chad. That's a contest for black drag queens."

"But I could win it."

"Have you ever heard about... cultural appropriation?"

Chad said, "No. Is that a contest too?"

"Look," I said, "I think you could win a drag contest. Maybe not Miss Ghetto Fabulous, but something. I think you could win. Maybe if you had some self-confidence." Dammit. I sounded like the idiots who were telling me I hated myself.

Chad sneered so seriously that he must have practiced this look in the mirror a million times. His eyes bugged out, brows up, upper lip jutted up, and teeth forward. "I guess you have not noticed, but I reek of self-confidence!"

"Oh, is that what that is?" I asked. "I thought that was Liz Taylor's White Diamonds." Not sure why I knew the name of that perfume.

"Shriek," Chad said. "I love Liz, but that toilet water should have stayed in the toilet. I only wear Coco water. Chanel."

"So, what is it then?" I asked.

Chad said, "Cha-nel. Shaaaaa-nellllll!"

"Sure," I said. "Chanel Number Zero. So, if you're so full of self-confidence, I'd say you're full of something else, but if you're so full of self-confidence, what's keeping you from winning a drag queen contest?"

Chad thought. I watched his face. Maybe he was thinking about self-esteem or pondering any flaw he might have. Or maybe he was evaluating his identity and his ongoing difficulty accepting his white roots. Finally, he spoke. "Well, for Miss Ghetto Fabulous… the competition is stiff. And, I wasn't born looking like a crack-hoe, I have to work at it!"

I thought about trying to have the cultural appropriation discussion again, but it's a challenging conversation with anyone, and near impossible with a narcissist. "What's the real reason?"

"No resources," Chad said. And the next sentence he said was just sorrowful, almost broken, like his mother had just died or something. "I just don't have the right clothes!"

"Chad! You have more clothes than Goodwill!" That just came out. But of all the things I thought Chad might have said about why he pranced around in drag at home all the time but had never gone out in drag in public, not having enough clothes would not have been my guess.

"But they're not THE clothes. They're not THE clothes," he repeated. "I've got old rags and hand-me-downs. I need designer gowns, one-of-a-kind couture, luscious, trendy fashions crafted just for moi! And hoochie-fied hot pants just like those." We stood in silence for a moment looking at the outfit in the Out of the Closet window.

"Why don't you try it on?" I asked.

Chad inhaled in shock. "I don't dare! Once I had it on, I could never let it go!"

"Just buy it," I said. "You make money."

"I'm a house cleaner!" Chad said.

"You're a house cleaner for the Getty's. Hey, I got on idea! Why don't you just lift something from the mansion and cash it out?"

Chad answered in a tone that was both smarmy and sarcastic. "Cause then I'd be keeping house at 850 Bryant. And I don't do prison well."

"Why don't you start your own contest? Like, Miss Flamin' Trailer Trash."

Chad looked horrified. "I am NOT Trailer Trash!"

"You're not ghetto, either."

"Besides, giving up on my dream of being named Miss Ghetto Fabulous, that would be just like quitting." Chad sighed and gave the hoochiefied outfit a final, wistful look. "Let's go," he said.

We left Out of the Closet and I started to steer Chad toward Hermann Street, blocks away from the delicious U.S. Mint. I knew Chad hated being called on his shit, but I rarely seemed to be able to stop myself. "Chad, have you ever been in drag in public?" I asked. Chad clammed up. It's like he put up an invisible force field. I had hit a nerve and I could feel it. I knew the answer. The guy dressed in drag in his house all the time and had never gone in drag in public. In a City where it was celebrated, how easy would it have been for him to strap-on some tiger print wrap dress and wear it to go get a freaking glass of Chardonnay? I was sorry I'd brought it up since I already knew the answer. "Sorry," I said. "I didn't mean to make you mad. I just don't get why you don't do what you want."

"Excuse me?" Chad said. "I'm exactly what I want to be."

That wasn't what I had asked, but I went with it. "A gay stereotype?" I asked.

"I am not a gay stereotype. Wait!" he said. He struck a pose, with both palms up and one arm extended, and he looked toward the heavens. "I am NOT a gay stereotype! That was much better!"

"If you like doing drag, do it. Who cares? Nobody in this City."

"You should mind your own beeswax," Chad said.

"Dude, you have a degree. In inter-frikken-national relations or something."

"Yum!" Chad said. "I met some hot Greeks in that program!"

"You should have it made," I said. "You're a straight white male. I mean, you're a white male. You could DO something with your life. So why haven't you?"

Chad stopped walking then started up again. "It's just... I've never succeeded at anything."

"Whose fault is that?" I asked.

"The world's!"

"And once the world gets its shit together and you succeed at SOMETHING, then what?" I asked.

"I'll run for political office!"

In my head I thought, "Oh gawd!" but I didn't say it out loud. We were coming up to the Mint. It was a modern fortress. I could see the cameras, the gates, and the spots where potential weapons could be aimed at us. "Say Chad," I said, "If someone, like me maybe, had the opportunity to take money, should I?"

"Do you mean steal?" he said.

"If you want to call it that," I said.

"Is it a business or a person?"

I said, "A business."

Chad said, "Then you should go for it!"

I said, "So it's okay if it's from a corporation, or a monster entity, but not if I was stealing from a person."

"No, that's okay, too," Chad said. "Under the right circumstances. Les Misérables. Jean Valjean and all."

"Have you ever stolen anything, Chad?" I asked.

"Of course! I'm only human," he said.

"What's the most you've ever stolen?"

"In cash, I stole two hundred bucks from my mom's purse."

"You stole from your Mom?"

"And I took a ring from one of my ex's. It was worth about five grand. Oh, but he deserved it."

Like I said before, ask the person who's going to give you the answer you want. Chad thought it was okay to steal, or maybe he was just saying anything and I was turning it into what I wanted to hear. Like, maybe I really was the modern-day Jean Valjean. Okay, probably not. I just needed to recruit him to help me.

Chapter 6 – The Mint that Refreshes

We were on the east side of the Mint. There was a formidable fence around the whole building and this side had lots of vegetation on it, including trumpet vines with blossoms. I wondered if the vines had been planted to tangle the feet of any intruder. I was looking for any weak spots in the armor when a hummingbird flew above the fence.

"A hummer!" Chad said. "I mean, the kind that flies." His reference being to the gay slang of a hummer being a blow job. "The hummingbird is my spirit animal! Whenever I see one, I know everything's going to go right! So, your idea – the stealing thing – it'll all work out. The hummingbird says so."

I looked at the hummingbird. They are very cool animals. I looked at its little wings vibrating. Hummingbirds are impressive, but I didn't know if they had much of a track record predicting the success of grand theft. The bird hovered near, then it flew right up to Chad. He reveled in it, holding his arms in the air, and had a little spiritual orgasm.

"Hey, if you like hummingbirds so much, why don't you catch one and put it in a cage in the house. Then everything would work out every day."

"You can't!" Chad said. "They die in captivity. If you put 'em in a cage, they'll die!"

"I know what captivity means!" I said.

"You know, the hummingbird has no natural enemy."

"I thought man was everyone's natural enemy."

"No. No enemies."

"I wonder what that feels like," I said.

"Beautiful bird! They have to be free! Just like me! Their spirits flutter with joy! Just like me. The hummingbird is all about beauty and pleasure and the magic of being alive! Just like me!" The bird had stayed right around Chad's head. "Oh, hello Mr. Hummer!" It looked like the hummingbird nodded at him and then it flew away. "What's your spirit animal?" Chad asked me.

Well, here we go again. Chad was hella stupid. I wanted to tell him he didn't get a spirit animal. That it was a sacred thing reserved for some native tribes, and as a dumbass white guy, he didn't get to look at a hummingbird, like it, and think he got to assume any traits that animal had. It was the cultural appropriation discussion again, but I needed Chad to help me so I didn't want to piss him off.

"Oh... I dunno."

"Well, what do you identify with? Or what animal is around you all the time?"

Gawd, I was a sellout. I was going to say something. I tried to think of an animal I identified with or saw. I guess it couldn't be the dirty, peg-legged pigeons on Market Street. The City mascot, Templeton, which was any fat, buck-toothed City rat, wasn't a good choice. "Uh, I dunno. Um... raven?"

"Raven?" Chad said. "Ick. That's all about death and mystery and misery and...." Chad looked me up and down and his tone changed. "Oh, isn't that nice. Raven. It's very, very, uh, survival-oriented."

I ignored him and tried to act like I just noticed the Mint. "Oh look, Chad, it's the U.S. Mint," I said.

"The Mint is on Market. Oh, you mean the money place. I thought that was on 5th."

"This is the new Mint. And it's not the bar. No karaoke. I think."

We had walked back to the Hermann side. We were near the guard station. I looked at the east side – that was impossible to enter. There was the fence, the meanest barbed wire you've ever seen, the cameras, and a two-foot raised barrier. What was I thinking? I wanted to break IN to a prison and my accomplice was a failed drag queen, one who couldn't even do drag in public. I walked up to the intercom and Chad followed. I could see a guard sitting in the booth, an older, heavy-set white guy. I waved at him. I buzzed on the intercom. I could hear it connect so I started speaking before he had a chance. "Hey, you stupid friend, can you give us a tour?"

The guy didn't respond at first but then finally said, "No tours."

"Get real, Barney Fife. I know there's a docent trapped in that rent-a-cop body! C'mon, it's not like we're gonna rob it." When I said rob it, Chad reacted, his entire body flinched, and his eyebrows went up. He had put two and two together to get five, and he knew what I wanted to do. The cop sat in the box and then spoke.

"You need to move on."

I took a few steps, Chad sort of shuffling along next to me, then I stopped and yelled to the security guard. "Make me!"

Chad said, "The man said go, A.J." That's when I sort of bolted up to the turnstile. I tried to stick my head through it, but it wouldn't fit. I yelled at the guard hut.

"Look cop-in-a-box," I said. Then I couldn't resist and said, "I'll have a double cheeseburger with large fries and –"

"I said move on," the security guard said on the intercom.

"Does anyone here have a sense of humor?" I asked.

The cop didn't speak for several seconds then answered. "No."

I took the few steps back to the intercom and leaned into the button. I put my whole bodyweight on it and wouldn't stop. Chad grabbed my arm and pulled it away. "What's wrong with you?" he said.

I caved and eased off the security hut. Chad and I started walking toward Market Street. I could see the gears cranking around in Chad's head and eventually he spoke. "Instead of this Mint, we should've gone to the Mint bar. The karaoke there is exceptional!"

"Well, Chad," I said. "I've lost."

"Lost what?" Chad asked.

"I officially give up. Let's go downtown."

"For what?" Chad asked.

"If I'm getting evicted from the City, I may as well go drink the last of my paycheck. And I wanna do it in a classy joint, not the Tik Tok Club." But, there was no last of the paycheck, so I asked Chad. "Do you have any cash on you?"

"Yeah."

We walked back to Church Street and waited for the "J," but I will say I get impatient because I've spent years waiting for the world's slowest transit. An old lady stood with us at the stop.

"Where's the J? Where?" I yelled.

"Why don't you try and get a regular job?" Chad asked.

"I'm gonna get some interviews," I said.

"You need to upgrade your wardrobe," Chad said.

"Upgrade. Right," I said. The sarcastic tone was thick. "These are the only pants I've got. Where is it? Why doesn't it ever fuckin' come?"

The old lady said, "You've got a bad mouth."

"That's not so," I said. "Fuck is an acceptable word,

you stupid friend. If I had a bad mouth, I would've said this train comes as often as you do, grandma."

The old lady said, "Well, I never!"

"Oh, I stand corrected," I said. "The J comes more often than that." And right when I shut my pie hole, the J was rolling up.

"Here it comes," Chad said.

The train came to a stop and the doors slid open. I had lifted up my right foot and I was about to step into the train when I heard someone yelling. There was a little, white dog running across Church Street. It wore a collar and was dragging its leash behind it. The pooch had the little dancing steps of a puppy and it was just happy as shit, a little smile on its fuzzy little face and a silly little tongue. It darted through the slow traffic, and cars hit their brakes and bikes swerved out of the little dog's path. It looked like a Maltipoo and the Malti's guardian was racing behind it trying to catch the little puffball, with cars braking to avoid hitting him too. He was calling, "Princess! Princess, no! Stop!" But it was a puppy and it either didn't understand or didn't care. My right foot was about to land on the entry step of the J. I looked at the train. I looked at the puppy. Well, I'm an idiot. I dropped my foot back to the street and ran to help the puppy.

"No!" screamed Chad. "We'll miss the J!"

I raced into Church Street and skidded on my knee, but I grabbed Princess up and pulled her close to me right before she got hit by a car. Princess's little tail was wagging, and she licked me in the face, unaware that she was two seconds away from going to the City puppy landfill.

The Malti's guardian ran up. "You bad girl! You bad girl!"

I didn't know if he was talking to the dog or me. He grabbed Princess out of my arms and split without even saying thank you. The J was still there, but I knew it was about to make the right turn and disappear from sight. I stood up and dusted myself off. I looked at my jeans. I'd ripped a big hole in the knee when I slid into second. Dang, these were my only pants! What kind of interview could I get now?

"What are YOU lookin' at?" I said to this fifties-plus broken-down guy, sitting on the curb. I had thought he was laughing at me, but he was just drunk and crying.

"Gawd, I hate myself. I hate myself! I hate myself for being gay. I hate myself for being a drunk. I hate myself for being broke…. Cause I can't buy anymore booze. And I can't drink myself to death. I hate myself for crying. And I hate myself for hating myself! And look at you! You're just like me. A self-hating queer. And you'll end up like me. Drunk and in the gutter!"

"Okay," I said. "Save me a seat. I'll be back in twenty years."

He kept crying and the scene left me troubled, though I encountered stuff like this every day. It only bothered me occasionally. The worst part though was when he said I'd end up drunk and in the gutter. Why did the world keep repeating what my father had always said would be my fate, that I'd end up dead, drunk and in the gutter?

I headed back to Chad and miraculously the J was still there. It was unbelievable, but I thought 'Hey! I had done a good deed. Maybe my karma was changing. I did something good and now something good happened to me. Maybe my life really could turn around.' Let me explain. The odds of a Muni bus or train waiting for someone was zero or less. Odds were much better that you stood at the bus stop and the bus rolled right on by without even flapping the doors in a mocking way. The train never waited. Chad stood next to the train, but the doors had closed. I knew it was too good to be true.

I walked over to Chad and he said, "You look like you saw a ghost."

I thought of the drunk in the gutter. "I did," I said. "The ghost of Christmas to come."

"The train's still here."

"Unbelievable. But the doors are closed." And just like that, like I had said 'Open Sesame' or something, the doors opened. We jumped on the train as quick as we could. And in that moment, I felt in every cell of my little body that things had changed. Things were going to be different now. Things were going to work out for me. Life had changed. The train waited. The doors opened. There was alcohol waiting at a downtown bar. I turned to Chad and said, "I'm making a decision, Chad. Right now. I'm not gonna hate myself. I'm not gonna end up in the gutter. I'm gonna be the person that the train waits for. I'm gonna win! The J waited, Chad. It waited for me. My life just changed. And you got to see it."

Chad was smiling and nodding his head and when I finished my little speech the train operator made an announcement. "This train is going out of service. This train is going out of service."

"Well, I guess your life didn't change that much," Chad said.

The passengers let out a collective groan and the doors slid open. I stepped off the train and as I did, the fog lifted, and the sun broke through. The raggedy gauze of the day was stripped away, and it was as if I stepped into a new, bright world. "What is it?" I asked.

Chad said, "That, my friend, is called the sun."

"Wow, so it DOES exist! Hey, who are you callin' friend?" I said.

I scanned the area as if it was the first time I had ever seen it. The broken queen was still sitting on the sidewalk and still crying. A guy was vomiting in the gutter. A homeless person was taking a dump at the curb. Across the street some shirtless musclemen were dancing in front of a bar that was blaring club music. You know, it was business as usual.

"It's the world of freaks and I'm the king!" I said.

"Guess that makes me the queen," Chad said.

I held my thumbs and fingers up and framed the Mint. It stood cold and gray in the distance. "You belong to me, cash-hole."

Chapter 7 – Enemy of the State...
Building

Kim told me what happened at the California Culinary College that night, and I could just see the whole thing play out in my head. All the students were standing in line, wearing those California Culinary College uniforms, with the checkered pants and the white chef's jacket, with the logo and their names embroidered on the left pocket side. The instructors were standing in front, all smiles, but you know how it is in a place like that. What looked like a smile was really just a bitchy, smug judgment of each student. Kim said all the students were talking softly when the lead instructor addressed everyone.

The lead instructor was Robert Bonner who said, in a French accent, that his name was "Robear." Robear Bonnaire. This was 2004 so you couldn't just jump on the Internet to search out someone's past, but every student in the class was confident he wasn't French. The thought was he was probably from Pittsburgh, moved to San Francisco, and reinvented himself as a French expat. Behind his back they called him Bobby Bon-bon. But he was in charge and he loved using that phony French accent.

He stood with his arms clasped in front of him and waited for the students to stop talking. Then he spoke, in his fake French accent. "I want to congratulate each and every one of you. You have all excelled. Make the most of your internships. I wish you luck. Bonne Chance!"

That's when Clark Peterson spoke up. He's a dick. Kim would go out for a drink with fellow students after class and, now and then, I would meet up with them. Most of them were okay, but a few were jerks. Clark hated Kim. I'm not sure why, but he was probably jealous of her. Kim was cool with most people. She was one of those 'if you have nothing nice to say, don't say anything' people where I was an 'if you don't have anything nice to say, you need to think harder' kind of person. So, Clark hated Kim, and just about everyone else and he always gave Kim shit. Anyway, Clark said, "Nice accent. Five bucks says he grew up in Daly City."

The internship everyone wanted was Quince. Quince was this posh little dining spot in Pacific

Heights, where the rich folks lived. The guy that owned it was Michael Tusk; I only remember that because of an elephant tusk. It was Italian, not that I could afford to eat there, but apparently Michael Tusk was the Michelangelo of pasta. The guy had worked for Alice Waters from Chez Panisse and Paul Bertolli. I didn't know who Bertolli was, but maybe his family owned Bertolli pasta. So, you were working with a guy who had worked for two top chefs.

Quince cost a fortune. It wasn't as expensive as The French Laundry, but for a tasting menu and paired wines, you had to mortgage your house and turn over your first- and second-born. But if you were lucky, and could get one of the few seats there, you might have the culinary orgasmic pleasure of placing the garganelli with Gorgonzola and beetroot on your neglected little tastebuds, the ones that thought gourmet pasta was a Cup O' Noodles. Quince had things like porcini mushroom ragout, or squid and artichoke salad. He made things like fresh ravioli stuffed with cauliflower and black truffle, roasted pork loin braised in balsamic vinegar, or lamb with two sizeable scoops of bagna cauda and delicately garnished with garlic scape and radish. It was enough to make you drool on the real linen tablecloth. You might wonder how a poor sap like me knew about Quince. Well, like all – even the poor – New Yorkers know about theatre, and like bumfucks in Iowa probably have forty different words for corn, San Franciscans know about food.

The Quince internship would train you how to make those high-end dishes, all the technique, all the coupling of ingredients, all the management skills – but there was one thing that Quince had that every student wanted. Michael Tusk was a chef. A chef who opened his own restaurant. That's what every chef in that program wanted, to open their own restaurant, to create their own signature dishes, and to suffer with the low profit margin – I mean, it's just a business that doesn't interest me. Too much work. But Michael Tusk - a chef - and his wife, Lindsay, had opened up their own restaurant. It just hadn't happened in the past. He held the key. He had the answer about how to do it and make it work. If you got that internship, you were on the road to opening your own restaurant. Everyone wanted the internship at Quince.

And one person was destined to get it: Kim. Kim was the best student in the program, and I'm not just saying that because I'm her roommate. I would be much more likely to trash her, like I did all my friends. But Kim was a gifted chef. She should have been a famous chef decades before, but it just hadn't worked out. Flour, salt, sugar, oil—it all turned into art when Kim molded it into a savory new dish. She was the best in the program, and everyone knew it; some were jealous, and some admired her talent. She had also worked hard. She'd learned new skills, brought in innovative ideas, and was always willing to do the grunt work as well. The Quince internship belonged to Kim.

So, the dumbass fake French fry cook, Robert, made the announcement. "First, the internship at Quince."

Clark leaned into Kim and said, "I guess that's yours, 'Miss Pinay.' Stupid bitch. Be sure to serve up your superior queer attitude."

Robert took a dramatic breath. "And it is awarded to Rochelle Washington."

Kim was shocked. So was everyone else. What just happened? Kim was supposed to get that internship. Rochelle was her friend, though, so she couldn't be mad at her. If anyone else was going to get it, she was glad it was Rochelle. Rochelle stepped forward, took the letter of introduction from Robert, and returned to line. The look on her face showed that Rochelle was also dumbfounded by the choice.

Rick Lenser, Clark's friend, said to Kim, "Guess you should've slept with him."

Clark added, "Maybe she did and that's why she wasn't picked."

Robert was as gay as a pickle in a peach patch and everyone knew it. The two straight white males from Clowntown were just razzing her.

Robert continued. "The internship at A16 goes to Clark Peterson." Clark stepped forward and took the letter with a smug grin aimed right at Kim, then returned to line.

Clark said to Kim, "You would have been great at A16. Oh, that's right. They don't serve lumpia."

Kim said she was angry and embarrassed and could feel her face turning redder and redder. She kept thinking of the different places that would be good for her: Michael Mina, Frisson, Aqua.

Robert continued, "The internship at Aqua goes to Kim...." As she heard her name, Kim stepped forward but then Robert said, "...Wong." Kim had to take a step backward to get back in line. She heard Clark and Rick snickering. The humiliation, the questioning of why this was happening. Kim was losing her mind.

Kim started saying under her breath, "Masa's, Masa's."

Then Robert said, "The internship at the State

Building…" and the whole class laughed. I will say the food at the State Building on Van Ness is terrific. The price is right, and you get a lot of food, but it's a cafeteria. An industrial cafeteria at that. It's not some hoity-toity San Francisco hot spot. Kim heard one of the students say, "That's like being a lunch lady!" And then Robert said, "Goes to Kim Macadangdang."

Clark said, "Dang, dang."

Kim hesitated. In her head she kept asking, is this real? Or is it some bad dream that she had the chance of forgetting over a morning cappuccino? She tried to make sense of everything spinning in her head. One of the other students gave her a soft shove and she stepped forward to get the letter before returning to her place in line. The other students chuckled.

"Mmm. State Building. That's good eatin'."

"You want fries with that?"

Kim told me she just stood there, frozen, isolated, her face glazed over.

Chapter 8 – Dire Straits

That night, I was in my room. While Chad's place was mostly Crate and Barrel, mine was just crate. I had a platform bed that I had made myself. I glued together a ping pong table I found abandoned on Mission Street, then I glued that onto some plastic milk crates. I didn't have a mattress, just a sleeping bag. Doesn't that sound cool? Let me tell you, the allure of being poor wears off in about three days. Sleeping in a sleeping bag on a hard ping pong table sucked. My room was pathetic. The only art I had on the wall was a North Beach Pizza Box I'd pinned up. I didn't have a dresser, just a stack of stolen milk crates. I was lying on my bed stacking up all the change I'd found – a little stack of pennies, a stack of three nickels, and a small tower of dimes. I had five quarters. Two dollars and sixty-four cents. It was around 10 PM when I heard Kim in the kitchen. I was hoping she'd brought home some leftovers. I smacked the stack of change across the room and got up.

Kim was filling up a glass with the wine from a box. Brenda, "The Mouse," was sitting at the table. She was a plain, nervous white girl with a moon face and she always looked shocked by everything, with her eyebrows raised and her eyes wide open. Brenda had a glass of the swill in front of her. I walked in and Kim grabbed up her glass and walked to the table.

She was yelling. "...doesn't make any sense! Is it because I'm Filipina? Fat? Queer?"

"Yeah, all those things," I said.

"I am so pissed!" Kim said. "My whole fuckin' life." She looked at me. "For once, you're right!"

"I am?" I said.

"Yes! We're treated like second-class citizens. Well, no more!"

I looked at Brenda, "Gimme that chair, friend." There were only two chairs in the kitchen. I got some of the box wine and sat at the table. Brenda moved and stood next to the counter. It always looked like she was hovering and quivering.

"Brenda," Kim said, and she used her head to point

to the bedroom. Brenda left. I took a sip of the wine. Well, at least it was alcohol. Kim took a massive gulp from hers. Then another. She had almost downed the whole glass in two sips. "The State Building!" she yelled. "My internship's at the frikken State Building!"

This didn't sound like a bad deal to me. Later on, Kim filled me in on the whole story. We never did find out what happened with the internship, but we decided Robert was out to get her, either she did something to him, or he was jealous. Anyway, like I said, the internship at the State Building sounded good to me. The food there was pretty good. "Maybe you'll get hired there," I said.

"No one wants to get hired there! It's a cafeteria! It's not even the Federal Building. At least the Federal Building has ambiance!"

"I dunno. Have you ever been in the post office in the Federal Building? I got punched there. It makes the Fox Plaza post office look sane."

Lynne came into the kitchen. "I could hear you yelling all the way upstairs!"

"Sorry," Kim said.

Lynne scratched her head and fluffed up her hair. She said, "I figured it was about the eviction."

"What?" Kim said. "You're getting evicted? I

told you!"

Lynne didn't respond for a minute, then she said, "You didn't tell her."

I decided it was best to chug the rest of the cheap wine before the glass was knocked out of my hand. Then I said, "You forgot to coach me on that... friend."

"Come on, Lynne," Kim said. "You can't evict somebody for one month's rent."

"It's six months," Lynne said.

"Six months?" Kim said then she was connecting all the dots in her head and you could see the calculations on her face. That's when she turned to me and said, "You haven't paid in six months?"

Lynne said, "This means – ."

"I know what it means," Kim said. Then the kitchen got quiet like a morgue. I could really have gone for some yelling about the Culinary College right about then.

Lynne said, "I'll let you two talk," and she left. I gulped and I felt the swallow travel down my throat. I knew this was going to be bad.

Kim and I were both sitting at the table and I patted her on the shoulder and said, "The Mint will solve all of this."

She took the last swig of her wine and said, "You lyin', punkass, piece of shit!" You could hear each of those commas as she spoke. "I'm not doing anything with you! Now I can't even move Brenda in without paying off your debt."

"Well, the good news in this is now you HAVE to help me, so you can stay."

"Forget it, jackass," Kim said, and she got up and refilled her glass with the box wine.

"There's no other way we can come up with that kind of money in two weeks," I said. "And if I get kicked out of the City…."

"I'll be kicked out of the City too," Kim said. "I can't afford anything else. Unless I help you pull off the stunt of the century."

That's when Chad strutted in, dressed as a butterfly. His wings were made from this rainbow parachute fabric and he wore a flesh-toned body suit and a glittery mask. Just in case we hadn't seen him, he strutted around the room again.

"Does anyone around here lock the door?" Kim asked.

"So. What do you think of moi?" Chad asked.

"Tryin' to talk here," I said.

Chad paraded around a little more. I checked out the wings, which were pretty cool. "Where'd you get those?" I asked.

"Oh, some gay para-glider misjudged his landing. I got this fabric for nearly nothing! I'm going to be on my friend's float! It'll be my drag debut!"

"You're gonna do drag in public?" I asked.

"I am! So hah!" He batted me in the head with one of the wings. "Hah!" He smacked me again. "I'll be fluttering on my Pride Parade float while you look on in envy! Our theme this year is: EMBRACE YOUR FABULOSITY!"

Kim looked at him. "Um. We're kinda busy right now."

Chad perched on the table. "So, who is it again you're gonna rob?" Chad had a knack for saying the wrong thing all the time, plus I couldn't believe that he couldn't remember something simple from the same day.

Kim looked at me like I was an idiot. "You told him we were robbing the Mint?"

"You're robbing the Mint?" Chad said. "What

are you gonna steal, the karaoke machine? Gads, don't do it during Pride Week. It'll set off a riot."

"Not that Mint, you idiot. The U.S. Mint," Kim said.

"I love the Mint bar! It is my party inspiration!" Chad had that lag to put things together. "Do you mean the place where they make the money?" Chad said.

"Yeah," I said.

"That place we went by?"

"Yeah," I said.

"Omigod, we're gonna be rich!"

Chad started dancing around the kitchen in his butterfly outfit, flapping his wings. I was thinking now that including Chad was a bad idea. And I wondered why I had ever thought it might be a good idea. I said, "I don't need any help! Except from Kim."

Chad dropped his wings low. "I wasn't going to help you steal it. I was going to help you spend it."

"Nobody else can know about this," I said.

"Especially Lynne," Kim added.

"Wait! I can help!" Chad said. "You'll need a disguise. To get in. That's where I come in."

I knew I had a reason for spilling a few beans to Chad. A disguise would be a good idea. And with all his clothes and makeup and stuff, he would be the guy to come up with a brilliant disguise. I looked at Kim. We nodded to each other. It was not a bad idea. Chad started strutting around the kitchen again, doing some sort of indecipherable dance with the wings.

"Gimme a little time for the genius to bake," Chad said. He stood in front of the kitchen window and admired his reflection. He turned from side to side, then checked out his ass and nodded. "Farewell, my little caterpillars. The next time we meet, you too will transform into a beautiful butterfly." Chad fluttered around a bit, raised his wings and struck a pose, then left.

Kim and I sat at the table. She stared at me, then looked away and sipped a little of the cardbordeaux. "Well," I said. "Is it a deal?"

"All my life I dreamed of being a great chef. Now that dream's gone bust. My career is dead. I'm about to lose my apartment. I'm in more debt than a small South American country. I guess I'm in."

"Start dreaming up a name for that restaurant," I said. "We're halfway there."

And just like that, it felt like my life was back on

track. Even better, I had a job interview the next day, and at that moment, I felt for sure I would get it. Then I felt a little flutter in my heart, it fluttered just like the wings Chad had built from the hang glider who had probably smashed into the jagged cliffs off Daly City and had instantly become a bag of bones. This was a little flutter. Not the heart flutter like you had just eaten two and half pounds of greasy ribs, but a different kind of flutter. It took me more than a minute to identify it. I started going through my mental list of common emotions. Was it schadenfreude? No. Weltschmerz? No. Damn those Germans, they had all the best words. Was it smug self-satisfaction? Not that. Was it relief from saving my ass from one more hellish situation? No. It took me a minute, but then I was able to identify it. It was hope. That was a feeling I hadn't had in a long time.

Chapter 9 – Audience of One

The next morning, I saw Kim and she had some serious bedhead going on. Her black hair was flattened on one side and was sticking out on the other. She was deep in the heat of passion and cranking up the thermostat five more degrees. She was rolling her head from side to side and I think I might have seen some drool rolling out of her partially open mouth. "Oh Baby! Oh Baby!" she said. She had her glasses on, but her eyes were closed and as she turned her head, her hair splayed out a little more. "Oh, I love you! I love you so much!"

Kim was lost, floating in ecstasy, merging as one with her true love. Right then, she opened her eyes and cheated a look east then west, hoping no neighbor had stolen a glance while she was snuggling Baby, her tricked-out Thunder Cloud Metallic Xb Scion. She relaxed in relief. No one had seen, except for me, of course, and she hadn't seen me. I wonder if she loved Brenda as much as she loved that SUV. Baby was parked on Dolores, no small feat that, and the spaces were tight, so she was hidden from any snoopy stares. She planted a wet, sloppy kiss on the bumper.

I popped up then, right next to the bumper, and said, "Gawd, I hate to break up this tenderlicious moment, but can I borrow Baby?"

"What?" Kim asked, and the sound indicated she had never been so outraged in her life.

"I'm late," I said. "I've got an interview in China Basin. I'll never get there in time on Muni."

Kim's mouth was half open. "I don't 'loan' Baby," she said. It was true. Kim had never loaned me Baby. Not once. She gave me a quick once over and said, "You wearin' THAT to an interview?"

I was wearing the only pair of pants I owned, the newly ripped jeans, and a t-shirt that read, 'I'm Not Gay, But My Boyfriend Is.' "These are the only pants I have!" I said. "C'mon. Please? Loan her to me. Just this once." I begged Kim to loan me Baby at least once a day.

"Besides," Kim said, "I'll never find a space this close to the house."

"I won't ever ask again," I said.

"Forget it," Kim said.

"Okay, I'll let you drive me. Then I won't touch anything on Baby."

Kim stretched her arms to show the beauty of the parking spot. "And there's two more days till street cleaning!"

"I promise, just this one time. It's a job interview. Money for rent. C'mon. Please." I knew my begging never looked cute or endearing. It was just pathetic. Well, that was that. I didn't get the wheels and I didn't get a ride. I stood on Church Street waiting for the J. I kept looking down the street to see if it was coming, and nothing. "Why doesn't it come?" Well, that was one interview I could kiss off. Luckily, I didn't want that job anyway.

Since I now had the day off, I walked over to Café Fleur. The new girl, later I learned her name was Daneetra, was working the cash register. I thought maybe my luck was about to change. She looked at me and said, "Triple soy latte?" Good memory, I thought.

I was a bit subdued because, you know, everything in my life seemed to be crumbling into bits, like a heavy fist on a house made of graham crackers. "Just a regular today," I said.

"Okay," she said, and she moved to the stainless-steel urn to pour the coffee. While she was getting it, I started counting my change on the counter and realized I was fourteen cents short. I couldn't even afford a cup of coffee. I hadn't brought all my change. I had to think fast. I would say compared to the average chump, I'm pretty sneaky. I faked a yawn and stretched my arms wide. As I did it, I slipped my hand in the tip jar and snagged a quarter which I confidently added to my pile of change on the counter. Apparently, from the side of her eye, Daneetra saw me. She placed the coffee on the counter. "Did you just take money from the tip jar?"

"No." When I said it, it came out musically. You could almost see the 'Yes, I'm lying' thought bubble above my head. "No," I said it again and this time, the sound was even worse.

"I think you need to go," Daneetra said.

I slid all my change off the counter, including the quarter, and I started to leave. Then I turned back and put on my best puppy dog face. "Can I have the coffee?"

Turns out, I didn't get the coffee. I started walking down Market Street, toward downtown. This wasn't the worst day of my life. It was just a typical day. Everything tanked. I walked past the shops, past the Safeway, where the Mint was sort of behind and above the Safeway, then I finally hit the Mint bar. Yeah, the façade was painted mint green. Ick. If you didn't know what it was, you'd think it was just a hole in the wall. Almost like a dream, I found myself placing my hand on the door handle, pulling it open, and walking inside.

The Mint had a mirrored wall on the east side and a U-shaped wooden bar with two levels. The karaoke stage was near the entrance, and it was small. The room had several small tables set up, and since it was so early in the day, they were empty. There were some interesting faux flames on sconces and a bubbly lighted wall fountain at the back of the stage. Monitors were hung throughout the room, showing the karaoke lyrics. It was not even noon yet, but people sat at the bar and, as always, the karaoke machine was fired up and ready to go.

I sat at the bar. I knew I would be ignored for several minutes and could just get my bearings. There was a twink on stage. I don't think that term was even around when this all happened, but that's what he was. A twink. And he was singing "I Will Survive." It wasn't a song I wanted to hear, as at that moment I really wasn't sure if I would survive. The kid had a whole choreographed routine and as much as I didn't want to like it, he was really good.

And as much as I questioned my survival, there

was something to learn in that moment. There were six people in the place: three guys at the bar, the bartender, me, and the kid onstage. But the twink was bringing it. He was performing like he was the headliner at Live Aid. He threw his head back, sashayed across the stage, tossed his arms wide with abandon. It was stupendous. Unforgettable. Transforming. And with the final notes, he was down on both knees giving it his all, doing a backbend, dripping with sweat. When he finished, there were a handful of claps, but I had learned something. It didn't matter if you were performing to an audience of one or one million. Give it your all. Because no matter how many people witness it, you can have confidence that you did your all and gave your best, Olympic-worthy performance and that's what counts. No one can touch it. Somehow, I knew it was important and that I was going to need this info. That's when the bartender came up to me. He was a fortyish, mustached white guy. "What can I get you?" he asked.

"Got any jobs?" I said.

"Bartended?" he asked.

"No, but I have related experience," I said.

"Like what?" he asked.

"I've been drunk."

The guy ignored that and asked, "Been to

bartending school?"

"Yeah," I said. How hard would it be to lie about that?

"Which one?" he asked.

I thought for a minute then answered. "Yale."

"How do you make a Hawaiian scream?" he asked.

I shrugged and said, "Kick him in the balls?"

The bartender said, "No skills, no job." He left and went to talk to one of the customers. My head was hanging down. I headed for the door, but I stopped at the stage area. I stepped up on the stage and picked up the microphone.

"Look people," I said, and my voice was so loud it was pretty obvious I didn't need a microphone. "I only wanted one thing from life."

I couldn't tell who was saying what, but from the handful of gay guys I heard, "Love!" and "Happiness!"

"Uh, get real," I said. "Money!" The small bar crowd cheered at that. At that point, I said, "I have no skills! I'm worthless! Useless! And worst of all – ." and that's when I tried to hit my falsetto. "I'm bro-hoe-hoe-hoe-hoke. Yeah!"

I heard the bartender say, "Another nut job on the

karaoke machine," and he headed for me.

"Thank you," I said. "I'll be here all week!" I ran for the door while the bartender was closing in on me. I rushed out of that place and began walking aimlessly, headed back to the Café, but I knew I couldn't go back there.

When I had walked half a block, I saw the U.S Mint. I went up to the chain link that surrounded it. I kicked the fence. On the west side, there was a lot of garbage that had been dumped—clothes, luggage, a broken computer monitor. I looked up and saw the security camera. I gave the camera the finger, and I hoped someone inside saw it. Here I was, on one side of the fence, broke and broken, and on just the other side of this fence, inside Fort Hard Knocks, were piles and piles of money. There was tons of money in the world, but none of it was mine. I thought about how Lynne was always talking about abundance. How everything we wanted and needed was available to us and how we already had everything we needed inside us to get what we wanted or needed. I really didn't see how it worked. All I saw was that there was plenty of everything and none of it was mine and I didn't know how to get it. I gave the security cameras the double bird. "Abundance, my ass," I said, and I headed home.

Chapter 10 – Kentucky Fried Fuck-up

Kim and I sat at the kitchen table. She was writing on a legal pad. She made a few notes. "Then how about Starbucks?" she said.

"Oh, not the Emerald Empire!" I said. "Plus, I can't stand the thought of being a bar-ista when there's no real bar."

Kim shook her head. "So, what's left?"

"Okay," I said. "I'm officially desperate. Fast food."

Kim had this look like she'd been waiting for me to finally arrive at this breaking point. "All right," she said. "What about McDs?"

"No," I said.

"Why?" Kim said.

"Cause it starts with muck."

Kim tapped her pen. "How about Carl's?" she said.

"I'm not working at Fascist Junior's," I said.

"Why not?"

"They wouldn't hire blacks in Oakland or gays in San Francisco."

"That was a long time ago," Kim said. "What if they changed?"

"No," I said.

"What about KFC?" Kim asked.

KFC. I thought. I pondered. Kentucky Fried Chicken. The Colonel. Wasn't every bite of that stuff 70% fat? "Don't they grow chickens with six legs?" I asked.

"I think that's Photoshop," Kim said.

"And they pump up the birds with hormones?" I asked.

"I think everyone does that," Kim said.

"And they tear the beaks off chickens?"

"That's what PETA says. Kentucky Fried

Cruelty."

I thought for twenty seconds. "Okay," I said, "That sounds good."

So, the next day I was standing on Church Street, waiting with all the other schmoes who were stuck riding Muni. It's funny. I can hold it and hold it and hold it and then I just crack. I yelled, "Damn! The only thing less reliable than the "J" is ME!" I was talking to no one and no one responded. No laugh, no dirty look, not even an accidental kick to the shins. All my teachers were right about one thing. Negative attention was better than none.

I went into the KFC on Guerrero at Duboce and the guy who interviewed me, his name was Luis, and he was all of eighteen years old. He was young and desperate, so he hired me on the spot. I don't mind working for someone younger than me, but I have to say it sucked to be pushing forty and having a kid tell me what to do. Oh, and he knew what he was doing, and I didn't. That may have been the worst part. He seemed nice enough and he was built like a potato; he must have been dipping into the thighs and mashed potatoes on his break. Like most young'uns, Luis had braces and acne and an eye for every busty woman who walked into the place. We were on the edge of the Castro, so there were more men checking him out than girls for Luis to ogle.

I got stuck working behind the counter and I had to wear a uniform. Luckily, the uniform was just a horrible striped polo shirt and a visor. I was not real hep on the visor. When I started, Luis showed me the ropes. "And this is the fryer," he said, showing me the fryer. Well shit, I wasn't a moron. I knew what a goddamn fryer was, and I could see the oil. When Luis turned, I tossed my visor in and watched it become a Kentucky Fried Chapeaux.

Luis continued the tour. "And here we have the – hey, where's your hat?"

"I didn't get one," I said.

"Oh," Luis said, then he pulled out another visor and forced it tightly on my tortured head. "There ya go!" he said. "Now you're KFC crew!"

"Terrific," I said. I can only guess being the boss is the worst thing ever. Having never been a boss, I can only guess. But having to pretend to be in love with the place and every single requirement, just thinking about it gives me acid reflux.

After the tour and the minimal training Luis asked, "Any questions?"

"Yeah," I said. "Can I get an advance?"

Luis looked shocked. I knew this kid could not give me an advance. I guess I just asked to annoy him. "No," he said.

"Well, can you loan me a few hundred?" I asked.

"Uh...." It appeared to me that Luis had never been asked to loan money to someone he really didn't know. From there on out, I needed to learn how to do this stupid, worthless job and not get fired. That was my solitary goal. I wasn't stupid. I just wasn't interested in investing my life force in some stupid job that was making money for the man. I had never really had a career goal. I don't know. Work in an office? I just figured things would work out. And they hadn't. Maybe somewhere in the world there was a place for my genius. It seemed pretty doubtful.

With the job, I was able to call a few friends and strongarm them into loaning me a little cash. I knew there would be big cash soon, but I had scrounged up several hundred and that night I went up to Lynne's apartment and gave her most of it, counting it off in twenties. "I'll have more next week," I said.

Lynne held the bills. "Well, the coaching seems to have made a big difference."

I kept telling myself to keep my big mouth shut and not say what I was thinking. She wanted to take credit when really, the promise of that sweet U.S. Mint money was what was keeping me in check. "Yeah?" I said.

"Yes," Lynne said. "You seem much happier. Less ready to blow every five minutes."

"Yeah?" I said, oh and I was ready to detonate right then.

"What about the plan?" Lynne asked.

And that was it. I exploded. Who blew it? Who told Lynne? "Who's been talking?" I said, "Chad? I'm gonna kick his ass!"

"You don't need to go ballistic!" Lynne said. "It's a good thing to tell others your life plan."

"Life plan," I said. "Yeah. That silly gay friend spilled the beans about my life plan."

"So, what is it?" Lynne said.

Life plan. Well, at this point it was to bust into the U.S. Mint and roll my fat ass in a wad of virgin uncut bills. And I was depending on a crazy drag queen to help me pull it off. "Life plan... I'll get back to you," I said, and I split. Lynne was calling after me, but I was long gone. I heard her yell, "What about the rest of the rent?"

Chad had told us he'd explain the plan that night so he met Kim and me in our apartment. Chad wore some fuck-me boots and a camouflage mini-skirt. I am always a bit concerned about anyone who considers camo print fashion; I'm always worried they're planning a coup. Maybe the only person who can make camo seem safe, from a military attack at least, is a good drag queen. Chad stood at the front of the room. He addressed the two of us like we were a filled stadium. "Ladies, ladies. And for once, they really are ladies!"

"That's questionable," I said.

Chad pulled out a car antenna he must have snatched somewhere, and he extended it to use as his teacher's pointer. "Ladies, behold! I have devised a plan worthy of –" he stopped as he wracked his brain. "Who was really big in the war scene?"

"I dunno," Kim said.

"Hitler?" I said.

Chad continued, "A plan worthy of Hitler-eeuuww! Wasn't he a Nazi? Ladies, I want a winner!"

"McArthur?" I said. "George C. Scott as Patton?" From the look on his face, I knew he had no idea what I was talking about.

Kim said, "What about Colin Powell?"

"Oh, yes!" Chad said. "He's a hunk! I have devised a plan worthy of Colin Powell!" Then Chad added a Mae West impersonation, "Ooh, he can invade my colon anytime!"

Kim rolled her eyes. I said, "Too much information!"

Chad tapped the antenna on the wall. It's not like he had a map or anything. "You'll rob the U.S. Mint on the day of the Pride Parade! I'll dress you up. You'll ride on the Fabulosity Float with moi! When you get to the end of the street, get into the Mint. No one will ever suspect two drag queens!"

The look on Kim's face. Chad may as well have be telling her she was pregnant. She didn't say anything and that said everything. Finally, she spoke. "Let me get this straight."

"Oh, don't get it straight, honey! Get it queer!"

Kim continued. "You want us. To dress in drag. Like a drag queen. And get on a float. In public. On Pride?" There was a pause as Kim gathered her thoughts. "Are you fuckin' retarded?"

Wow. I had never heard Kim use the "r" word. There was only one word worse than the "r" word, and that was the "n" word, and I had definitely never heard Kim use that. For her to use the "r" word, she was obviously troubled by this plan, but I guessed that she was on board.

I was confused. "But how do we get into the Mint?" I asked.

"Well," Chad said, and you could tell he was trying to think up some sort of answer because he furrowed his eyebrows and his eyes were moving from side to side. "You create a diversion."

"Like what?" I asked.

"You know," he said. "A diversion! A big diversion!"

"I think the two of us in drag is a pretty big diversion," Kim said. "This is absolutely stupid."

"What kind of diversion?" I asked.

"Oh, for Goddess sake!" Chad said. "That's your job!"

"Yeah," Kim said. "You come up with the diversion."

Well, I was no Colin Powell, no McArthur, no George C. Scott. But I had earned my Ph.D. in Bullshit and I felt that made me qualified to come up with a million-dollar distraction. I could do this. "Okay," I said. "I can do it."

"Now, let's focus on the important things. First: your gown."

"I don't have a gown," Kim said.

Chad put his hands on his hips and wagged his little head. It was such a gay stereotype, but he was so good at it that I just had to enjoy it. "Oh, I am so very shocked!" he said with ten pounds of sarcasm. "Step one, a gown. You must get a gown! I want you to be comfortable, so you'll be picking it out. Now, moi, I prefer a bodice so tight I have to be sewn into it, but I want you two to be comfy."

I had no idea what he was talking about, but he just kept yapping. "Something glamorous. Yet attuned to your personality. Hose and shoes too. And you need it by tomorrow!" On the last word, Chad abruptly slammed the antenna to its smallest position and put it in his pocket. "And now, I'll exit, fabulously." Chad extended his arms and started his fabulous exit, walking the runway like Miss America until he bumped into a plastic trashcan. That kind of busted up the look, but he regained his regal stance and exited.

Kim used to smoke and had quit, but right then I could see it in her eyes. She wanted a cigarette badly. "Dude," she said. "Are you gonna wear a dress?"

"Friend," I said, "I'm desperate. If it'd make me rich, I'd wear a wedding gown."

"Dang!" Kim said.

Did you ever hear a bad idea and right when you heard it, you knew it was a bad idea, but you were so desperate that a bad idea sounded pretty good because at least it was an idea? Inside of you, there was a voice shouting, "Don't do it!" while the rest of your brain nodded "yes, this'll work." Well, that's what happened at that moment. Right at that moment, none of it made sense, but we had our camo mini-skirt marching orders. We both needed to find a drag queen outfit… one that was good for a dyke!

Chapter 11 – You Must Remember This

The next day I grabbed a cup of coffee at Fleur and sat at one of the outdoor tables. I'd been watching Daneetra. She'd seen me, but luckily didn't say anything about pilfering from the tip jar. I was getting ready to leave. I wasn't exactly flush, living off borrowed cash right now, but I had to redeem myself. I pulled a five-dollar bill out of my pocket and I paraded around, in between the iron tables, banging into a few chairs along the way and no doubt gaining a few big fat bruises.

"Say what's this? Oh, it's Mr. Lincoln! Mr. Five Dollar Bill. Not that lame, wooden-teeth-wearing President barely worth a buck. No, this is Honest Abe. Our sixteenth… or seventeenth President. Four score and all. The man with the beard and the stovetop hat. The man who freed the people. The gay President!"

I worked my way over to Daneetra and flagged her down. "Scuze me, Scuze me," I said.

Daneetra was wiping down a table and didn't look too happy. She stood with her hand on her hip, rag in her hand, looking at me.

"This is for you," I said, and I slapped the five-dollar bill down on the table she had just wiped.

Daneetra didn't snatch up the money the way I would have. She looked at it and she made a face I would describe as unimpressed. Then she spoke. "I hear you come in here. Almost every day. You've never left a tip. Might have stolen one. My co-workers say some days you've barely had enough money to pay for a basic cup of coffee. And today, you tip five dollars."

"Yup," I said.

"Why?" And damn, the sound of that was so harsh. It was like she'd said fuck you, but she'd said why.

"I'm finally getting the money I deserve. Big Money. Chedda chedda. Moola. You can call me Mr. Moola."

"Is that your name?" she asked. At this point we hadn't even formally met.

"It's A.J.," I said.

"A.J.?" she asked. "For A Jackass?" Not a bad guess, I thought. She shrugged and said, "I'm Daneetra."

"Hi," I said.

"Hi," she said. It was all pretty lame. You see those movies, like Bogey and Ingrid Bergman and they're at the airport at night and words come out of their mouths like a symphony spinning across their vocal cords, sketching a love story in the mist and the best I could do was "Hi."

"Um, I was wondering, if uh, maybe. Well, you know. I think you know what I'm saying." This was definitely no Casablanca. There was no lookin' at you kid. There was no foggy airport farewell. The only Resistance in my internal movie was my own. I was no Bogie. There was no "Play It For Me, Sam," then I started thinking about the song from Casablanca and spaced out.

"Actually, I don't have the slightest clue what you're saying."

I hesitated. It was that clutch second. I could have jumped the fence and ran. But I stayed. "I thought maybe you'd like to do something sometime."

"Like what?"

"I dunno. Maybe get a cup of coffee."

"I work in a coffee shop all day. The last thing I want to do when I'm done is get a cup of coffee."

"Okay. Well I dunno. Go out?"

"With you?"

"I'm coming into a large sum of money soon," I said. I don't know why that came out. It seemed to be my only selling point.

Daneetra said, "So what?"

"Then I could pay. Your way."

"I have money," she said.

"I know that. Working at a coffee shop and all."

"I'm a grad student."

"Oh, what are you studenting – uh, studying?"

Daneetra winced. That's the best word I can come up with. She pulled her upper lip tight and up, not showing teeth, but she looked like she was ready to bite me. "Philosophy," she said. She took a beat then continued. "Look, I'm not interested in… capitalists."

"Oh, I'm not a capitalist," I said. "I'm a criminal! A petty thief!" Okay, so this may not have been my best selling point. Sometimes I open my mouth and shit comes out.

"I need to get back to work," Daneetra said, and she turned her back on me.

I walked out of Café Fleur and as soon as I was out of there, I punched a parking meter and started screaming. It really hurt my hand and impressed no one. Plus, I should have said grand theft, not petty theft. I was not going to be a small-time criminal. I was going to be big-time!

I walked back home. I had decided to give Lynne a little more of my newfound cash. I don't know why. Really, I should have kept my paws on every dollar I had. But there I was at her door, counting ones into her hand.

"Forty-eight, forty-nine...okay, forty-nine. Rent. It's great, right?"

Lynne took the cash in her hand, then straightened it. "Yes, it is. But you haven't even caught up on one month," Lynne said. "I know you're working on the life plan. And have you been using the word *friend*?"

"I sure have, you crazy friend." I must admit, Lynne's advice to use the word friend in place of bitch was brilliant.

"I've been thinking. Maybe if you stopped being so homophobic, you'd get somewhere. That and the self-sabotage," Lynne said. For a lot of reasons, I was regretting coming back to the house and talking to Lynne. When people say totally stupid things to you, what are you supposed to do? Talk shit back? Leave? Clock them in the head? But before I could consider decisions, I was ranting.

"Homophobic? I'll tell you who's homophobic. The assholes who treat me like a second-class citizen!"

"Eleanor Roosevelt says, 'No one can make you feel inferior without your consent.'"

"Fuck your friends! Whadda they know? Oh, and in that case the word friends actually meant friends. I may hate myself, but I don't know if that makes me homophobic or just me-phobic." If I didn't talk so fast, I would have registered that she had said Eleanor Roosevelt, you know, Franklin's gay spouse.

"A.J., you've got to find a way to love yourself," Lynne said.

"Oh, I learned how to do that by watching lots and lots of porn."

"You know what I mean," Lynne said.

"Sorry, I'm just not into the goddess and the moon and all that new age crap."

"Nobody said you had to be. But there's so much energy in the feminine. And you're cutting yourself off from it."

"What's the feminine got to do with me?" I asked.

Lynne sighed. You could read frustration in the sound. "Everyone's got both sides. Even men have a feminine side." That's when she leaned over and touched my forearm.

"Don't touch me. I told you I don't like it."

Lynne didn't say anything for half a beat then spoke. "Bet you'd like it from the girl at the coffee shop." I was pissed. Damn that Kim. She just couldn't keep her mouth shut.

"Listen, friend," I said. "If you're gonna play with dynamite, you better be ready for a big kaboom." And if I had been closer to the door, I would have slammed it for emphasis, even if it wasn't my place. I split and started walking down the interior stairwell and there was that funky smell of dampness that's in every San Francisco flat, whether there's carpeting or not. That acrid smell was exactly how I felt. I wished I had kept the forty-nine bucks. Oh well. At least I had kept several bucks reserved for the gown.

I walked over to the State Building Cafeteria and I could see Kim inspecting the food on the grill. The grill worker was looking at her like she was crazy.

"…that's the point when you can put light

pressure on it. Make sure it's fully melted, but be careful to not crush the bread," Kim said.

The grill worker looked at her. "It's a grilled cheese," he said.

"Exactly," Kim said. "It's someone's meal. This is going to nourish someone. Treat it like it's a gift to your family. When you make something, whether it's a grilled cheese or a fried egg, act like it's the last meal you're ever gonna get to make for your grandma."

The grill guy looked at her and I don't know if he really cared or not, but he nodded his head and said, "Okay." I was really glad at that moment that Kim didn't work at KFC. I didn't need to be guilted about making my granny's last meal a lousy bag of McNuggets.

Kim saw me and came over. "I'm at work. And no, I can't give you any free food."

"I got money now," I said. "Plus, I get all the cold wings I can eat at KFC. I came by to make sure we're going shopping tonight."

Kim made this face with a wrinkled brow and lemon-lips, her mouth all scrunched up like she had a stuck popcorn husk cutting into her gums. She finally said, "Yeah." Right then a customer walked up, a white guy with khaki pants, a polo shirt, and a badge hanging from his belt, you know, the standard issue office worker uniform.

"Hey! Are you the head cook?" the guy asked.

I could see Kim's self-esteem was shot. She knew the guy was about to dump a big ass complaint. "Yeah," she said.

"That was the best burger I ever had! Thanks!" And he meant it. And I watched Kim and right then something shifted. She stood up taller and looked the guy in the eye.

"Thank you," Kim said. The guy walked away, and Kim watched him leave and you could see the gears going off in her head; she was re-creating her self-value.

"Hey, Kim," I said.

"What," Kim said. Not a question, more like a final response and she didn't look at me.

I whispered. I didn't want anyone to hear me. "What's the feminine?"

"What?" Kim said.

"What's the feminine? Lynne's always talking about it and I don't even know what it is," I said.

"Hmm...well, you know. The side of yourself

that's receptive. Intuitive. Nurturing."

"No wonder I've never heard of it. Are you ever feminine?" I asked.

"Sure. With Brenda. When we—" I cut her off.

"Hey, my stomach's already upset," I said.

Kim kind of leaned toward the glass partition that separated us. She picked up a burger flipper. "Okay, when I'm cooking. It's nurturing. And I get to serve."

"You get to serve. Food. You get to serve food." I was trying to make sense of this.

"I mean be of service," she said. "Cooking, serving people…."

"Be of service," and I pondered, as much as I could ponder. "Okay, it sounds like the feminine is getting used, getting duped, getting taken."

"And there's creativity. Creativity is feminine. And speaking of that, did you come up with a diversion yet?"

"Workin' on it. Just a little more… diversification. Okay, thanks. I gotta get to work. After work we'll go shopping for the ball!"

"Great," Kim said, and she went back to the grill. So, there it was. No one knew what the feminine was.

Or they did and it was something no one wanted to discuss in depth, like how they avoided discussion of their daily bowel movement or what it felt like to take out a tampon. I was shit out of luck in the feminine game then I remembered – Chad. If anyone understood the feminine, it had to be him. But my musing on the societal infliction of gender norms would have to wait. I had to get to Kentucky Fried Chicken.

Chapter 12 - It's Lonely at the Bottom

L et me tell you, this was not a good day. I got to
KFC, I was only about ten minutes late and I
thought that was pretty good. I was packing coleslaw
in these little individual containers. Okay, I will say
I find it awfully hard to pay attention in general, and
putting shredded, wet cabbage into a little tub, well,
you didn't have to be Einstein to do that. I lined a
bunch of the Colonel's baby bowls up, then was
spooning it out, and I might have been a little sloppy,
and maybe I might have missed a few of the
containers and I may have possibly splattered some
of it on the counter. And the floor. I scooped up a
small pile that had fallen on the counter and put it in
the container. I will say in my defense, I was wearing
serving gloves. I was wrapping things up and I took
a glance from right to left. Luis was nowhere around.

And I stuck the serving spoon in my mouth to get the last bite for myself. Without fail, Luis walked up right then while I still had the spoon in my mouth.

Luis had that look on his face, the one I imagined parents gave when you had failed them. And remember, this kid was eighteen years old. I was thirty-eight. When I looked closely, I could see he was shaking his head "no," but just slightly. He was showing his teeth, but not in a smile, sort of a teeth-with-braces frown. "Man, you suck," he said. "You can't do anything right. And you don't care. I'm gonna have to can you, man."

"Fired? I'm going to get fired? From KFC?"

"Yeah," he said. "You don't know how to do anything."

This was the worst news ever. I had finally reached the pinnacle of the bottom, getting bounced from a fast-food gig. Then I thought of Kim telling that grill worker to make a grilled cheese sandwich like it was a royal feast. Maybe that was what had been missing from my entire work life. I just didn't give a shit about work. But I did like money, and right now KFC was the means to the ends, and it would let me keep my apartment and plan my miraculous caper of robbing the U.S. Mint. Would life be different if I actually tried? I mean, if I didn't just pretend to try, if I would actually really try to do a good job? This was like trying to hold the entire meaning of eternity in my head at once, and my soft noggin' was about to explode. I took the leap.

"Then show me," I said.

"What?" Luis asked. I am going out on a limb here, but I'm guessing in his expansive management career he had never had to fire anyone and didn't know how to handle it when they wanted to stay.

"Show me," I said. "I want to serve. I want to do it right."

Luis stood there and looked all around the shop, everywhere but at me. It must have taken all he had to fire me and now he didn't know what to do. "I dunno," he said.

"Please! If I get fired, I'm a dead man," I said. I was surprised at the sound of desperation in my voice. Pathetic, and I was begging for a burger-flipping job, no burgers involved.

Then Luis said, "Okay. But only cause I'd like to get back some of the money I loaned you." Well, I had squeezed a twenty out of him, though he had been hesitant the first time I asked.

Then Luis started from scratch. He showed me the fryer, how to fry the chicken, how to use the cash register, how to make the biscuits, and how to pack stuff up. For the first time in my life, I was a diligent student, struggling under his tutelage, but continuing. At the end of the day, I needed to pack more coleslaw. This time it was different. I was in The Zone. I was an artist, the Yo-Yo Ma of slaw packers!

Luis watched me in awe. "Wow! You pack coleslaw better than anybody! You're like the Randy Orton of coleslaw!" For whatever reason, I actually knew Randy Orton was a WWF champion wrestler.

"We're a team!" I said. "What's your name again? Doesn't matter. I'll just call you Colonel. Wait, Colonel Luis, that's it."

We knuckle bumped. Luis looked at all the little packed coleslaws then he smiled and showed his teeth again, which he rarely did because of his braces. Bu this time, it was a smile and I could see a little light in his eye dance. I don't know if he was happy about the slaw or happy he was able to train the troubled student. I looked at the line of packed coleslaws. This had been different. When I packed them, I had infused them with the desire that whoever ate that coleslaw loved it. That each bite of crunchy cabbage with a dressing that was both sweet and a hint of tartness would make the eater know they were valuable. That someone cared enough for them to get a good meal. I wasn't playing anymore.

"Wow!" I said. "It's the first time I've ever done anything well."

That evening, Kim and I headed over to this used clothing store on Mission I knew that specialized in slutty items. Kim had already found some stuff, but I just kept searching through the racks. This was not going to be easy. I had found this one dress I liked, it was silver lame with only one sleeve, but it was a hundred dollars. A hundred dollars! For one dress. That only had one sleeve. Who knows what it would cost if it had two sleeves?

"You're taking forever!" Kim said.

"It's hard for me!" I said.

"I've already found two things! You've got nothing!"

I examined another slutty dress. My little head was spinning around. There were just too many choices, and I was getting overwhelmed. "I just... don't know."

"Here, I'll help," Kim said, and she zipped through the rack. In seconds, she pulled out a black dress with gold thread running through the fabric. "Try this one."

"I dunno," I said, looking at the dress. It was pretty short.

"We don't have all night! Put it on!" Kim was getting to the end of her fuse.

"It's so low cut...!" I said. I wore a t-shirt and jeans every day. I didn't know if I had it in me to go out in public showing the goods. But it was only $29.95.

"Just shut up and put it on!" Kim said.

I stumbled into the dressing room and put the dress on. It actually fit, but I could not wear this thing, it was really low cut. I stared in the mirror. I could not reconcile the image staring back at me. If this was the feminine, I wanted nothing to do with it. I didn't go around showing my legs, and I wasn't used to material that clung to me and showed my body. All of a sudden, I sort of saw my mom staring back at me. If I had longer hair. I missed her. I barely remembered her, but I missed her. I wondered how different my life would have been if she had lived. I had to shake off that feeling of seeing her in my own reflection. Luckily, Kim was yelling for me to come out. I finally slid myself out with the dress on. It was seriously so low cut that it landed at my crotch.

I timidly snuck out. I couldn't believe I was standing in public in this trampy hoe-frock. Most of my bra was peeking out and you could see my boxer shorts. This was a plunging neckline that plunged like an arrow and landed right at the pubes. "There is no way I could wear this!" I whispered to Kim, "It's gonna show the shorthairs!"

That's when a salesclerk came up to me and said, "Excuse me, ma'am. You can wear it like that if you want, but you've got it on backwards."

It turned out this was a backless dress and I'd put it on backwards. That's why it was so low cut! More evidence I was not cut out to be a feminine female, or maybe any kind of female. I lived in the stupidest city in the world, one where any freak could fly their flag of independence and declare any allegiance – gay, bi, trans – just as long as you weren't a Republican, and I couldn't even fit in here, in the two-layer candy box of decadence. So, I bought that slutty, backless dress and another one that was more of a gown, and we headed home, bags in hand.

"Hey, we're set," Kim said. "You should feel good now."

"I spent money on clothes!" I said. I started calculating in my head how much I had spent, when really, I should have bought some new jeans to replace the ripped ones. "Man," I said. "I coulda bought about 99 beers – hey! That reminds me of a song!" We made it back to the apartment in record time.

Chapter 13 – Life's a Drag

We dragged our bags up to Chad's apartment. He had us sit on the couch and gave each of us a diet soda. I wasn't into drinking chemicals, so I let it sit. Chad excused himself and we sat there for a while. Then, as abruptly as he had disappeared, Chad returned, wearing a new outfit, and strutting out from his bedroom.

He was now wearing a leather dominatrix outfit. He had a leather cap jutted to one side. He had meticulously painted on some red pouty lips and applied red eye shadow. I'd never seen red eye shadow before. He had on a leather teddy that laced up and he had some fake boobs stuffed inside. Over the teddy, he had on a pleated, leather Catholic school girl skirt. Of course, he had on some leather fuck-me boots, a new pair. He wore a big wig that looked like it had been snatched from Dorothy Lamour in her prime. He struck a pose, standing in the doorway with one arm on the door jamb and the other on his hip. In that hip-holding hand, he had a riding crop. After the pose, he slapped the crop in his hand. He walked around the room sizing us up, then he stopped at the front of the room and announced: "And now: Chad's House of Charm presents: Runaway Runway! I'm your hostess, Fashionista!"

"Looks more like Fascistnista," I said. You gotta remember, this was 2004 and Chad was basically now running his own two-buck drag race. It was a homegrown version of what RuPaul would launch five years later.

"Silence," Fashionista said. She poked me with the riding crop. "How's the Kentucky Fried Gig?"

"Oh, looks like I was born to work at Gay-F-C. Amazingly, it's not 100% awful. Plus, all the cold wings I can eat!"

Kim said, "I didn't know they let you have free food."

"They don't!" I said. "But you know - when no one's looking - I can fit a whole wing into my mouth and still talk. The thighs are impossible."

Chad made a full circle turn, flipping the rear of his skirt up while he spun around. "Here," he said.

"Let me set the stage." He took a standing halogen light, turned it on, and aimed it like a spotlight on himself. Then he started singing, "Don't You Wish Your Girlfriend Was a Freak Like Me." It was a popular song at the time, and he was slapping the riding crop on us, on himself, then exclusively on his own ass. You know, when you get into these sorts of deals, there's always going to be a show before you get down to work. Finally, he stopped with the singing and the slapping and focused the lamp on Kim and me.

"Welcome! I'd like to welcome everyone to our little fete!" he said. And there it was again. That thing that gay guys do better than anyone else. Like the guy doing karaoke at the Mint, Chad was performing for an audience of two, but it may as well have been two million. And this was somehow related to the coleslaw. And Eureka! It dawned on me. He cared. He cared about what he was doing. It mattered to him. I had seen so little of this in my lifetime. And Kim cared about cooking. And I had seen a glimpse of it when I was in the Zone, packing coleslaw. Had I ever cared about anything or anyone before? Yes, when I was a kid, I had a little turtle. They stopped selling those little turtles because they all had salmonella. My dad got it for me not long after my mom died. Its name was Star and it fit in my hand. I loved that turtle. Until my neighbor's dog ate it. But at one point, I had cared. I was realizing there were things inside me, emotions, capacity, knowledge, that I didn't even know existed. Then I snapped back into listening to Chad. "Now it's time for the first annual Miss Wannabee contest. We have two lovely contestants who both Wannabee girls!"

"I dunno know about that," I said. Kim was first and Chad ordered her into his bedroom to put on her outfit. When she came back, she had changed into a white satin slut suit that was at least two sizes too small. She had on this platinum wig that came down to her shoulders and landed in a severe cut at the ends. With her slouchy, lumbering walk, she marched to the front of the room. Chad stood there. With his arms crossed, one hand held his chin and the other held the crop. He stared and said nothing for many seconds. Finally, he exploded.

"Omigod, it's a Pilipino blowup doll!"

Kim wore these two-inch white heels, and she was teetering on them. I felt like Chad and I were swaying from side to side with her. Kim had put on the world's reddest lipstick and still wore her butchy Buddy Holly glasses. Chad pulled off the glasses, but I really couldn't tell if it was better or worse.

Chad shouted, "Binge eating Barbie!" Then he shouted like a pirate. "Avast ye maties! The Great White Satin! She's about to blow!"

Kim wasn't impressed with his Captain Ahab impression. She said, "Enough with the fat hating." Fat shaming wasn't a term then, but Chad was conducting some serious fat shaming. Kim sat on the couch, and I went to change.

I picked out the evening gown. It was not satin, but the fabric was silky. I guess it was soft like that because it was really a tacky polyester, but I liked the colors. I hadn't tried it on in the store, but I really liked the pattern with swirls of orange, purple, and pink.

I scraped my feet along when I came out. I had bought some shoes that had a tiny heel, they were called kitten heels. You gotta figure, I could count on one hand the days I hadn't worn sneakers and I had big old monkey feet, wide at the toes and narrow at the heels, so nothing fit. I walked out. I was mostly looking at my feet, though the dress was really long and covered them. I was trying not to trip on the dress, but I did look up and saw Chad's face. I would use the term "Horror-Filled" to describe it. He looked at me, then he discreetly reached and turned the halogen spotlight off. You could hear my shoes scraping on the wood.

"Oh," Chad said. "You look just like Miss America! Like Miss America ate a gallon of rainbow sherbet and threw up!" Chad hit me in the head with the riding crop. "What were you thinking! I hope you saved the receipt!" He slapped the crop in the palm of his hand.

I tried to take the last few steps to the front of the room. "I'm gonna trip on the caboose," I said.

"That's a train! In your case, that's a train wreck!" Chad stomped around the room in his femmy military boots, looking me up and down, doing his evaluation. He took the neckline and pulled it forward and inspected my boobs. There wasn't much to see.

"When did you have a mastectomy?"

"I didn't," I said.

"Oh," and I don't even really know how to describe the sound of that Oh. Sniveling, punk ass son of a bitch might capture it. Dudes. Straight or gay, they all seemed to think women's boobs should be the size and shape of a bocce ball. Then, suddenly, and dramatically, Chad dropped his head in his hands, like he had the Superbowl of migraines. Kim and I shared a glance.

"Okay," I said. "The whole idea was stupid. Let's just forget it."

Chad now had his chin on one fist. The other arm, dramatically extended, palm up. He was drawing life force from this disaster. He uttered a sort of gasp, then spoke. "My whole life has brought me to this moment. Somehow, I will pull all my skills… my knowledge, my color sense, my fashion genius, my intense fabulosity, and, coalescing all my talents – and some hard work on your part – we might, we just might pull this off."

He looked at Kim. He walked around the couch. He ran his hands through the platinum wig. "For you… something more exotic."

Kim adjusted herself. "Hey man, I'm not gonna play into all the stereotypes men have about Asian women."

Chad walked to the front of the couch and took a good long look at her. He said softly, "I think ya better."

Then he walked over to me and was sizing me up, patting that riding crop in his hand. "And you. I think a June Cleaver look."

"Oh, hell no!" I said. "I was goin' for a neo-Pamela Anderson sorta thing."

Chad ignored every word that came out of my mouth. He said, "Plus, your last name's Billingsley! Just like the real June Cleaver, Miss Barbara Billingsley!"

"Barbara Billingsley. That was my mom's name."

Chad said, "I guess that makes you 'The Beaver!'"

I held my fist up at him and said, "I'll show you 'The Beaver!'"

Chad put the back of his hand to his forehead. "Please don't! If I have to see a real one, I'll faint!"

Kim said, "You looked at Rachel's."

Chad sniffed and stiffened. "That's because that he-she tunnel was man-made. And I had to get a look." Chad thought for a second. "Lucky for you both, I have something from my private couture that can meet your needs. But first - a christening! You need a drag name."

Chad placed his hand on my head. He closed his eyes and sucked up some universal inspiration. "You'll be Lotta," he said.

"Lotta?" I asked, pretty resistant to that old lady name.

"Lotta Baggage." Next, Chad considered Kim. "For you... the perfect name. Inspired by my idol. Coco."

Kim liked this. "Coco Chanel!" she said. "That

works."

"Yes, I said 'inspired.' In your case, Coco Puffs."

I was ready for Kim to go ballistic on him, but she didn't seem to mind that name. "Did I do okay with the makeup?" she said. "I asked the counter girl for help."

Chad winced. "Why ask a counter girl, when you can ask a queen?" He placed his hand on his heart. "I would think you both already knew how to properly apply the warpaint."

"Why?" I asked. "No one ever took care of me. My mom was dead. My dad started drinking cause my mom died. Nobody made me oatmeal or played Candyland or showed me how to put on makeup."

"No one showed me how to put on makeup either," Chad said. "And yet," and he made a grand, stylized hand flourish around his face. With no break, he transformed back to Fashionista and gave me my marching orders. "Now, take off that vomit gown!"

I was pretty pissed that I'd bought this stuff and was going to end up wearing something Chad already owned. Maybe I could trade in the gowns and get a new pair of jeans… or I could trade in the gowns and get a couple of Cape Cods…. Chad ran into his room and you could hear him pulling stuff from his closet. I started taking the gown off while Kim polished off her soda.

"After a while when no one takes care of you, you take care of yourself," I said. "You learn not to trust anybody else, not to need anybody else, and not to hope for anything better." Kim didn't respond, but I was pretty sure she agreed with me. Her parents had been older, and I knew she had to fend for herself.

Chad rushed in with a handful of dresses and accessories. He grabbed me like I was his toy poodle and pulled off the vomit gown then strapped this fifties style dress on me. It had a floral, pastel print and a full skirt. It was nothing like what I would have picked. He put this coiffed wig on me, and it was sort of a June Cleaver look. Chad was patting himself on the back with every choice. "Yes! Yes! It's all coming together. The toad is transforming into a prince... cess. You only need one thing to finish this look."

"A blowtorch?" I asked.

"June Cleaver always wore pearls. Oh, but I'm fresh outta fresh water." He glanced toward Kim.

"Don't look at me," Kim said. She was still stuffed in the white satin number.

"I've been trying not to!" Chad said.

"I got some beads like that." I don't know why I

offered anything. It's just those pearls. I hadn't thought of them in a long time.

"Mardi gras trinkets and Jerry Springer baubles won't do. You need the real deal," Chad said, but I was already out the door.

It was night and I was fishing through the milk crates that made up my dresser when I spotted the box. It was old and crushed. I opened the box up; it had that fuzzy stuff that's in jewelry boxes. I pulled out the string of pearls and darted out.

I ran back into Chad's apartment and there was Kim in the center of the room, now dressed in a silver rhinestone halter top gown. It was really form fitting and Kim had a bit of a beer gut. "Damn!" I said. "It's like a mirrored ball got knocked up!" I really don't know how Kim put up with us.

I held up the pearls. "Like these?" I asked.

Chad snatched the pearls from me and said, "Brilliant!"

"Where'd ya get those?" Kim asked.

"My mom left 'em to me," I said. "Well, she was dead, y'know, so my dad gave 'em to me."

Chad reveled in the pearls. He held them up to himself, giddy. He slid them across his tongue, then he started licking them.

"Hey!" I said. "What d'ya gotta lick 'em for?"

"They're real!" Chad said. Then he walked over and ceremoniously put them around my neck, fixing the clasp.

"I've never had 'em on before," I said.

"You never put them on?" Kim said. "Not even for play. Or sentiment?"

"Well, maybe I wore them once." Something about those silly beads seemed to transform me for a minute, and I invoked a bit of the domestic diva. I touched the pearls and did a little walk around the room.

"Omigod! June Cleaver's boyish sister! Gilda Lily!" Chad said. Gilda Lily was really crossing the line for me, but Chad just kept on going. "Good news Pinocchio, those pearls have made you a real girl!"

Chad got in my face and checked out the pearls. He was digging them. "I guess your mom did help you out, after all."

"Do ya think we can pass?" I asked.

Chad looked at us. "Well, it'll be a pity pass," he said. "Sashay a little."

I didn't know what he was talking about.

"Walk and swing your hips," he said. I did and even I knew it was frightening. I felt like I was playing an old lady, the mayor's wife or something, in a mediocre fifties musical. Kim was doing some sort of prance and it might have even been worse than my moves, if that was possible.

"Think June Cleaver, not meat cleaver," Chad said.

I would describe my attempts as 'mincing about.' And I had a look of total concentration, you know, that face some people make when they're dropping a deuce. Kim seemed to be doing some sort of "I'm a Little Teapot" dance or something. If Dante was around, he would have taken a few notes for Inferno.

Chad stopped us. "Well, YOU won't be winning Miss Ghetto Fabulous, but you just might pass the fifties sitcom test. Now, I'll enroll you both in Chad's School of Charm. I want you to practice walking in those heels twice a day for at least fifteen minutes. And start building a lip-sync routine to your favorite pop diva tune!"

He put the riding crop under his arm and clapped his hands. "Home now. You need your beauty sleep!"

"I have beauty sleep apnea," I said.

Kim and I walked to the door and just as I opened it, Lynne walked down the steps. I slammed the door and jumped back into Chad's apartment.

"What is it?" Chad asked.

"Lynne. I can't let her see us." And I realized I had run to our place in that dress and Lynne could have seen me. I could always lie. Tell her I was exploring the feminine. Yeah, she'd fall for that.

"Oh, gawd no," Kim said. "She can't find out about this!"

"I can't let her see us dressed like this," I said. "Let's wait a minute. Hey, take these off me," I said, and I pointed to the back of my neck, indicating the pearls. Chad started taking them off.

"I can't believe you never wore these," Chad said.

"Maybe I did wear 'em. Once," I said.

Kim snorted and I knew she hadn't meant to. "When?" she said.

"At the prom," I said and the second it rolled off my coated tongue, I wished I had lied and said something else.

"YOU went to the prom?" Kim said. Though punctuation would make that look like a question, it wasn't. It was a statement. A statement of disbelief.

"Yeah," I said. "I went with this guy I knew. Ted Roper. Everyone called him Ted Raper. He was gay. It seemed safe. The two of us going. We could both go. And enjoy it. And have the same experience as everyone else. Y'know, be like everyone else for one night."

"Gads!" Chad said. "Next she'll tell us he popped her cherry in the backseat of the Taurus!"

"Was it fun?" Kim asked.

"No," I said, and it was almost inaudible. This was a sign to the others as there is absolutely nothing inaudible about me.

"Why not?" Kim asked.

"Ah, you know. We got harassed by some dumb fucks."

"You're gay," Chad said. "That's a given."

"They chased us out. Into the parking lot. They grabbed Ted and they beat him." I had rarely shared this story, and I didn't know why I was telling these two now. They were both definitely my friends; I just wasn't into sharing my personal information. It was better, and it was safer, to keep everything inside.

"Did they hurt him?" Kim asked.

"Mmm. They fractured his skull. He was in a coma for months."

"Did he live?" Kim asked.

"Yeah," I said, and I knew I sounded really defensive. "Yeah, but he was never the same. Part of me wishes I'd stayed and tried to stop them. The rest of me is glad I didn't help him. Let's be real. They would have raped AND killed me."

Chad hadn't been talking, but he had his hands on his chest and now spoke up. "You abandoned some poor gay man to a bunch of hoodlums, and you want ME to help you?"

"I couldn't DO anything!" Dang, I was pleading my case and throwing myself on the mercy of the court. "It's not like it was a Matthew Shepard thing."

"It was a lot like a Matthew Shepard thing," Chad said. By the way, Matthew Shepard was this young kid who was beaten and tortured and left to die in Laramie, Wyoming. Laramie is about twenty miles south of Bumfuck, Wyoming, the place that I knew was ready and willing to kill me. This poor kid was killed because he was gay, so comparing anything I had ever done to killing Matthew Shepard was a low blow.

There was a silence and we all avoided eye

contact. I stalled as long as I could, and I knew I needed to speak up. "I would've helped him if I could."

"Sure," Chad said, his voice brittle as ice.

"He's probably okay now," I said. "Medicine. It's changed. Stem cells."

"Of course," Chad said.

"Anyway, that's the only time I wore the pearls," I said.

"No wonder your mother died on you," Chad said.

Kim tried to make things better. "It's not like you beat him up," she said.

"Yeah. I can tell you one thing, though," I said.

"What?" Kim said.

"Prom sucks," I said. "Hey, I think the coast is clear now!" We snuck back to our flat. Later I realized we should have just changed back into our street clothes!

Chapter 14 – The Nobel Piece of Chicken Prize

The next day, I was heading to work, well, really, I was just screwing around before work and I was walking down on South Van Ness past the Dudley Perkins Harley Shop. It used to be in Hayes Valley, but they moved to Van Ness.

I looked in the window and there was the object of my affection, a small red Harley. There was a time in my life when I felt it was important to know everything – make, model, specs. But as I'd gotten older, I just didn't give a shit. It was red and it was my size.

I had sat on that model bike before. Harleys, they're not like other motorcycles. You slide into the seat of a Harley like a hand eases into a well-fitted glove. Once you wrap your legs around that monster, it feels just like fucking. I've been on a lot of bikes, but only sitting on a Harley felt like that. All I had done was sit on the Harley in the Dudley Perkins shop; I'd never taken one out on the road. Who knew how delicious it felt to fire that little red demon up and have that roaring power between your legs as you cruised down 280?

That red bike owned me. I was mesmerized. But it cost like ten grand. Ten grand may as well have been a million dollars. But if it worked out, if we went into the Mint and got a stack of uncut bills, I could be riding that puppy.

And then I was off in a little fantasy, first imagining a montage of me on the bike from all different angles, then close up. And all of a sudden, the engine fired up and I was riding the bike, zipping through the city, tearing down the highway. It was a lot like a terrifically lame music video with me as the star.

Next, I was at a biker bar. I pulled up on my mean red machine and the bikers poured out of the bar, like ZZ Top's angry family reunion. These guys were some mean sons of bitches. They wore leather jackets, torn jeans, and bandanas. They had long beards, ones where the hairs had gone out of control and stuck out at odd angles. I knew there was probably some mustard from six months prior lurking somewhere in that face bush. The bikers formed a small mob as I got off the bike. One pounded his fist into his palm, ready for a fight. They circled around me. I took off my helmet and stood there. Then they nodded their heads in approval of my bike and welcomed me into the bar.

Then I was in the Mint, rolling in uncut sheets of money. I will say, I did have clothes on for this. I rolled back and forth on those sheets and with each turn another sheet adhered to me and soon I was a big, green, money burrito.

All of a sudden, I was standing next to a glossy real estate agent who pointed out a lil' all-American house with a white picket fence and everything. I wore a suit and tie made from money. I took a couple of all-knowing glances at the house, nodded with a "this'll do fine" look and peeled off several uncut sheets of bills. The real estate agent smiled and handed me the key. I opened the gate for Daneetra who was wearing a bright spring dress. She wore sunglasses and carried a small designer dog, a Yorkie, I think. I straightened my tie with an homage to Rodney Dangerfield and followed.

Then I was back at the Mint again. All my friends stood in line as I doled out the uncut sheets to them. Kim took a sheet, then Lynne, then Chad. Apparently, I had purchased a lot more friends because the line went out the door, but the money was an unending pile, and I handed out sheet after sheet after sheet.

Then I was back at Gimme A Brake and I rode that

red Harley all through the shop, revving it up as loud as I could. I drove around the cars, on top of the cars, I even drove on the ceiling. Sammy hopped on the back and we spun donuts around Jerry.

Then I was back at the U.S. Mint. I did a swan dive into a big metal hopper, the one that prints out the money. Sheets of three-dollar bills churned out with my face on 'em.

Then I was back on the Harley, trekking up a soft, brown hill. It was a little rolling hill and as I went up it, I would have to say I felt free. My hand on the accelerator, pulling it toward me and increasing the speed, I felt in control of my life for once. Then I realized I was riding the Harley up a woman's body, the hill was her breast. That knocked me out of my little fantasy and there I was standing in front of the Dudley Perkins Harley Davidson store. I looked at the glossy red gas tank, the chrome V-twin engine, that lascivious leather seat that you know if you stuck your face in it, it would smell like leather, and maybe a few other things, and I smiled.

I walked into work. Things had changed at KFC. I was good at what I did. Maybe scooping up fast food wasn't what I wanted to be good at, but dammit, I was a champ. I had precision, focus, and I cared about what I was doing. I had never experienced such a thing. I could cap off a soda, box a dinner, and swoop up three chicken sandwiches. If Mihaly Csikszentmihalyi had discovered flow in a bag of breaded legs, if Jim Thorpe made instant mashed potatoes, if there was a Zone at KFC, I lived in it. And the most very odd thing was, it was very satisfying. What would the word be? Was I proud of what I was doing? Well, there wasn't a Nobel Prize for working at a dumpy chicken coop restaurant, but I was ready to submit an unsolicited nomination. For myself of course. So there I was, livin' it up at the Colonel's. Luis was checking the chicken in the fryer and I was on the counter.

"Two more minutes on the wings! Start packing the slaw!"

I had turned to listen to him and nodded. Then I turned back to the counter and there, right in my face, was Daneetra. What can I say? My worst fear had come true. I was horrified and humiliated. Neither of us said anything.

"Let's go out there!" Luis yelled.

I kept my head down and asked, "May I help you?"

Daneetra said, "This is where you work? This is your big money?"

I was completely mortified. I just started doing

my spiel. "Maybe you'd like the manager's special today? It's a barbecued chicken sandwich."

Daneetra thought she was funny and said, "Does it taste like chicken?"

"Tastes like shit," I whispered. Then I smiled. That's when I saw Luis was standing right next to me. Yeah, he had heard me, and he had a big frown on his face.

"I highly recommend the manager's special," Luis said. He grabbed me by the sleeve of my polo shirt and pulled me around. "What're you doin?" he said.

"Oh, did I tell you I have Tourette's? That just happens sometimes. Do you know what Tourette's is, Luis?" This was a kid, eighteen, who was interested in girls, cars, and watching TV. Of course, he didn't know what Tourette's was.

"Is it like having your period?" he asked.

"Yes," I said. "Yes, Luis. It's exactly like that."

Luis didn't know what to do and the mention of a period seemed to just trouble him. "Well, watch it!" he said, and he moved away from the counter, and towards the back.

I started talking to placate him. "I will say the coleslaw has been packed with precision! And a little

TLC. TLC for KFC!" Even I will admit I was an idiot.

Luis was gone and there I was facing Daneetra. "I just wanted some mashed potatoes," she said. I gave her an eye and shook my head, just slightly. "Some baked beans?" she asked. I gave her another high sign to stay away from the beans. "What about corn on the cob?" Facially I hemmed and hawed. The corn was passable. "Okay," Daneetra said. "A corn on the cob."

I put on gloves and grabbed the corn on the cob. Then I got all frazzled looking for a bag. The bags were always right there, but where were they? Now, now when I needed the bags. Were they missing? Were they in front of my face and I just couldn't see them? I was out of the zone, and I had lost my mojo. Damn!

Luis yelled, "Fries are up!" I ignored him. He yelled again. "I said, 'Fries are up!'" I still stood at the counter, frozen. He walked over to me and said, "When I say, 'Fries are up' that means you leave your station and remove the fries, like we practiced." He picked up the fry cage and docked it. "Am I clear?" he asked.

"Yeah, you're queer," I said.

Luis grabbed me again by the shirt sleeve and

dragged me to the side. He was a whole lot bigger than I am, so it was easy for him to railroad me anywhere.

"What did you say? I thought we were a team."

"We are a team. Because you are a total friend." Luis liked that I called him a friend. If he only knew it was my code-switching for bitch. "Luis, do you like girls?"

"Yeah," he said and nodded.

"So do I." He kind of reacted to that. You could see the comprehension gears going off in his head. "And I kind of like that girl out there, so give me a break." Luis was still holding my sleeve and he finally let it go and went to the back. I turned back to Daneetra.

"Work's a bitch," I said quietly and I smiled, and she smiled back.

"Well, I guess you're a Kentucky Fried capitalist. But at least you're not the man." We laughed and I found the bag for the corn on the cob.

Chapter 15 – Freedom's Just Another Word…

I was sitting at the kitchen table, gluing rhinestones on my purse, and I'd like to point out that's something I never thought I'd say in my lifetime. Kim was making pancakes. "Last night I realized something. Doin' this - it's not about the money," I said. "Wait, wait, wait. It IS about the money! But it's also about…" and trailed off as I tried to figure out what is was about. I could pick up a slight whiff of the oil on the griddle.

"What?"

"I dunno..." I said. "Winning?" Was it winning? Was that what it was? I was pulling different ideas into my head and accepting or rejecting them. "If we pull this off, I won't be a loser."

"Damn," Kim said, and she flipped a pancake.

"Damn." She was silent for a few seconds. "And if you can change, YOU, someone who's wasted her entire life, spent every moment angry, spent every second of every day hating herself, if YOU can transform yourself, then anyone in the world can!"

"Yeah," I said. "And if I can't?"

Kim stood to think. "Then things stay the same."

"Oh, that's the worst possible thing ever," I said.

Kim still stood there. I started to worry the pancakes would burn. "Did ya ever feel like…" and she stopped for a second. "There's an answer somewhere in the universe. And if you only had the key, life would be easy and good."

"Wow. The cosmic lock, dude," I said.

"Yeah," Kim said. "The cosmic lock. And if you could pop the cosmic lock, you could do anything."

The kitchen was silent. Was there a cosmic lock? And if there was, was there any possibility it could come to two gay girls in San Francisco in the year of 2004? Or was it out of reach for all? Why was it that some people seemed to have such an easy life, everything came their way, work and love and money? And even those lucky souls bitched that life was unfair. But for me, or Kim, two people who really had experienced a challenging time in all those areas, why?

Why couldn't an easy, interesting life just happen? This is where I usually started thinking that at least I had food and housing and water when a lot of the world didn't, but let's be real, if I lived in those other places, I would have been executed the moment I opened my mouth. I lived in San Francisco and there was a lot of money here and a lot of opportunity… I just didn't know why it was always six feet out of my reach. Maybe there was a cosmic lock and all I needed to know was how to pick that lock.

"I can do it," I said. "The Mint is our only way out. It's our cosmic lock. I can come up with a diversion. I can get in and out. I can win for once. And that's gonna make me free. Not that useless 1776 free, free on the inside."

"Free for real," Kim said, and she flipped a pancake high in the air.

"Yeah," I said "Free. It's almost like doing it, pulling it off, the success of it, is almost more important than the money. And please note, I said almost."

"Man!" Kim said. "And you wouldn't just be popping the cosmic lock for yourself. You'd be unlocking the struggle for everybody gay. I mean, if YOU can turn your life around, there's hope for everybody. Even straight people."

"Whoa!" I said. "I just gotta come up with a diversion. It's that easy! We DO have a plan! That's the plan. And when we're in, we roll up those uncut sheets of money!" I used my hands to show how thick that fat roll would be. "Like a poster. No, a small rug. Wait, a big rug. We can do it!"

"Then I can tell those shits I go to school with to kiss my fat ass!" Kim said. And she said it again and turned a pancake with each word. "Kiss. My. Fat. Ass!"

I laughed then said, "It's like that flag said, 'Live Free or...' um...."

"Or die," Kim said.

"I forgot that part. I got a lot riding on this. You're lucky. You already got your shit together. You got a career. A girl. There's nothin' you need."

All of a sudden Kim seemed really sad. "Yeah," she said.

"What?" I asked. "What did I say?"

"You wouldn't understand," Kim said. She looked completely sullen. She abandoned the pancakes, something she never does, she never leaves food out. She turned off the grill, and she left the kitchen. And I sat there, alone, wondering what I had said that caused Kim's reaction. Oh, and I ate all six of those pancakes. Delicioso!

Chapter 16 – Pride and Joy

It was Saturday, the day before the Pride Parade and you could tell because the City was getting really crowded. Like I said, because of the whole marriage equality deal, they expected an especially large crowd this year. There were rainbow flags everywhere, the special occasion leather had been busted out, and even this early I saw the bar across the street had turned into bear country.

The day before, Friday, they had the trans march. It was the first one. I know, you think that stuff has been going on forever, but it had to start sometime and 2004 was the first one. There had been a transgendered woman, Gwen Araujo, and four guys murdered her and dumped her body. There were a few trials on this, two of these guys had slept with her and when they found out she was trans, they murdered her. Oh, and even as I write this, this shit just continues. People think it's okay to kill somebody because they're trans or gay. Ridiculous. In that trial, they asked for a hate crime and the guys who killed her used the gay panic defense, said they panicked when they found out she was trans. But, hey, they didn't kill her when they had sex with her and I don't think you could really be panicked about it later, and that says premeditated all over it. Bottom line, they killed her. It wasn't panic. They were humiliated and they were out for payback. The community was pissed, and the trans march started. There were about 2,000 people at Dolores Park for the first one.

It's hard to explain Pride Week to people who haven't experienced it. It is a balance between ritual and out-of-control fun. Today, they would set up the pink triangle on Twin Peaks, and tonight was the dyke march. The Pink Saturday party would happen in the Castro that night, but it was basically already happening by the time I got to Café Fleur in the afternoon.

I was sitting at an outdoor table drinking my coffee. The place was packed because of the 850,000 or so extra people in the city. I had to share the table, something I never cared to do. These two guys in their thirties sat at the table with me. I wouldn't have minded listening in on their conversation, but there were so many people jammed into the place, I was having trouble eavesdropping.

Right then Daneetra walked by, and she had a tray with some dirty latte cups. "How's the coffee?" she asked.

"It's beautiful," I said, and I felt like an idiot and I could feel my cheeks blush, something that rarely happened. "I mean it's good. Very... caffeinated."

Daneetra said, "Can I ask you something?" and she almost had to yell.

"Yeah!" I yelled back.

"Wanna go to the parade with me?"

Wow. That was a question I was waiting my whole life for someone to ask me. And now I was gonna have to say no.

"Yeah, I do!" I yelled. And I must have had a sad little frown on my face. "But I can't."

"Why not?" Daneetra yelled.

I had been putting all my brain power into coming up with a diversion and I hadn't thought of anything for this. I hadn't expected anyone to ask me to go to the parade, so I didn't have an excuse ready. "I gotta work," I yelled.

The look on Daneetra's face was like a mom who had just caught her kid in the worst lie ever. "Instead of going to the Pride Parade," she said. "You have to work. At Kentucky Fried Chicken." Daneetra lifted an eyebrow, rolled her eyes to the side, and smirked.

"No, something else," I said.

Though there were tons of people around, I could feel the freeze. Daneetra was giving me pure ice. "I see," she said. "Look, it's okay. You don't have to tell me her name or anything."

"No, no," I said. "I'd really like to go with you. To the parade, or anywhere. I'd really like to go with you. It's just... I'm... I'm <u>IN</u> the parade."

"You are?" Daneetra asked.

"Yeah," I said, and I wasn't even lying, which kind of shocked me.

"You're a dyke on a bike!" Daneetra said.

"No. I'm on a float," I said.

"Which one?" Daneetra asked. "I'll look for you!"

Gawd, I couldn't tell her that. Plus, I don't think I knew. Okay, I did know, but I couldn't have Daneetra see me in that silly domestic diva dress. "Uh..." I said. "I guess I'm not on a float."

"Hmmm," Daneetra said. "Well, enjoy your coffee."

"Daneetra, wait," I said, and I grabbed the sleeve of her shirt and she nearly dropped the tray with the dirty dishes on it. She pulled away.

"Thanks, I'm not into liars. Or drama."

"What if it was really, really good drama?"

"Pass, honey. I'll pass," Daneetra said, and she moved to another table.

"Yeah, but will I?" I said to myself.

I went back home, and I went to Lynne's flat. Lynne was giving me a coaching session and it was perfect because I was starving and with every coaching session, there were snacks involved. There was a tray of fancy crackers and cheese and granola bars and I was gobbling them up.

I said to her, "But what if your whole life was wrong – everything about you was wrong? You don't know what that's like."

"I completely know what that's like."

"If I had money, I'd be okay. Money is what I need. I'll do whatever it takes to get money. And then I'll be free."

"Freedom doesn't come from money," Lynne said.

"But money doesn't hurt," I said.

"Freedom is really about being everything you are and being okay with it," Lynne said.

I scooped up as much food as possible. "Sure," I said.

"When you really let yourself experience unrestricted freedom, then it doesn't matter what you're doing. The power of your life force, that's what makes you free," Lynne said.

This actually caught my attention. "It doesn't matter what you're doing? What if you're a thief?"

"Then you have to be the best thief there is, revel in the robberies, steal more than anyone! Remember, connecting with your life force – the universe – that's what makes you free."

I started stuffing snacks in my pockets. "Yeah, that's what I was thinking," I said.

Lynne leaned back on the couch. She reflected. "You are the universe itself. It's all inside you. It doesn't matter what people say or think, if you know: I value myself, then you won't want to do anything negative, like be a thief."

"Yeah," I said. "I just wanna be rich. I don't care how."

"If you're rich and hate yourself, you can't be free," Lynne said. Lynne got up from the couch and got the smudge pot and smudge stick. "Sounds like somebody needs a smudge!" She started to fire up the smudge stick.

"No, thanks," I said. "I already smudged in my pants. Anyway. I'm leaving."

"Remember, start by embracing the feminine," Lynne said.

"That shit gets old," I said.

"Now you can start substituting 'stuff' for 'shit.'"

"That shit gets old too."

"Going to the Pride Parade tomorrow?" Lynne asked

"Yeah," I said, "but only because they don't have a self-loathing parade."

I went back to my place. It was Saturday night. We were so close. I stood there standing in front of the open fridge, just staring in there, apparently hoping for some food to appear. Kim came in and tossed her backpack on the kitchen table.

"Where you been?" I asked. "I was getting worried." Kim ignored me. I opened a plastic container from the fridge and smelled it. Whatever was inside was no good. "No Brenda?" I asked.

"No," she said.

"Good," I said.

"We had a long talk today," Kim said.

This was some news I had been hoping for. "Breakup?" I asked.

"Not that kind of talk," Kim said.

"Well, you musta done all the talking. I've never heard two words out of her," I said.

"She's afraid of you," Kim said.

"I mean, when you have sex, does she talk dirty? Does she scream when she comes? Or just squeak and eat cheese?" I asked. I made the mouse squeaking sound. I found some spaghetti in a plastic container. Jackpot. I chugged the spaghetti from the container.

"Stop," Kim said. "We went to my parents' house. That's what we were talking about."

My mouth fell open and it was full of spaghetti. "What?" I said. "Nay and Tay! And you lived to talk about it! Dang, how many years has it been?" I said. I knew a little Filipino – Nay, Tay, and that guni-guni meant hallucination. That was about it.

Kim was mad. I could see it in her face, but she also started to move differently when she was mad. It was heavier, like she was lugging her body around. "I had to see them. I knew you wouldn't understand."

It turned out when I said she had everything, I was wrong. There was one thing she really wanted that she didn't have, and that was a connection with her parents. Having them accept her and Brenda. She told me about going to her parents' house in Daly City. Yeah, she drove out there, knocked on the door, but there was no answer. The door was unlocked, so she went inside. She told me it's a middle-class house, with an old sofa and an old TV. Right when you walk in there was a small shrine set up for her cousin who had become a bishop or something. All sorts of pictures of him in the bishop hat and a bunch of Catholic stuff. You know, Kim hadn't set foot in a church in a decade or two.

She called, "Perfecto," and her father's head appeared from around the door frame. "Nay," Kim called, then her Mom walked out too. Her parents were near tears. Kim pulled Brenda over next to her. "I'm home," she said. No one moved and they all stood there looking at each other in one of those typical, awkward family moments.

I was amazed Kim had gone out there. Plus, she had the guts to take The Mouse with her. It made me wonder if I would ever talk to my father again. Nah, probably not. I couldn't imagine me tracking him down, driving out to see him, trying to fake some sort of connection with someone I didn't like. He would ask, "How are you?" and I would say, "I'm almost 40 and not dead and in the gutter yet." But Kim had reconnected and that was pretty amazing.

"Did you come up with the diversion?" Kim asked.

"Yeah," I said. "Mostly." I stood there.

"You don't have a diversion, do you?" she said. I just looked down. "A.J., we're fooling ourselves. Because we wanna believe. This isn't gonna work. Besides, just getting into the place, that's not big enough to pop the cosmic lock. I don't know what it would really take to change our lives. To get the whole world to accept people just for who they are... gay, straight, big, small, black, white, whatever."

There it was. Kim brought up the possibility we couldn't do this. I really had avoided thinking about it. The fantasy of it all working out, it had been so alluring, but what the hell were we doing?

"Dude, I just wanted to survive. Get enough money to – you know – survive. That's all. Maybe the cosmic lock is somebody else's job...."

"We have nothing," Kim said.

My stomach was fluttering, and it wasn't the old spaghetti. I was scared. I might have been scared about trying to pull off this caper, but I was also scared that my life might continue on the same shitty trajectory it had been on for nearly four decades. "I can't give up again. This time, I'm gonna screw up like a man."

"Woman," Kim said.

"Something. I've never followed through with anything in my life. This time, even if I fail, I'm gonna do it. I'm gonna finish something even if it kills me!"

"It might," Kim said.

"So, we have no plan. No ideas. No skills, no ideas," I said.

"We do have one thing," Kim said.

"My pearls," I said.

"A gown," Kim said.

"We're fucked," I said.

Chapter 17 – All Dressed Up with One Place to Go

Today was the day. Sunday. June 27, 2004. The Pride Parade theme was Out 4 Justice. Today was the day that was going to change my life. I tried not to think about it as I drank my morning coffee. Yeah, I did actually have coffee in the house and drank it there on occasion but going to the coffee shop was my sole social activity.

I had to get dressed. I still had butterflies in my stomach, but I went in and put on the Mrs. Cleaver dress with its full skirt and large flower prints in pink and yellow. I had a big beehive wig, another accessory Chad had loaned me. I put it on. I put on the makeup, the foundation, the eye shadow, the bright red lipstick. All this crap that I had ignored, avoided, or sworn off. It really was crazy, I didn't look like myself, but maybe a goofball sister. It actually was a great disguise, no one could tell it was me.

I looked at myself in the small hand mirror I had. I balanced it on the milk crates and checked myself out. I growled. "You are one hot suburban meatloaf! Embrace the feminine! With this bod, who wouldn't?" I took the hand mirror and gave it a big smooch. My red lips left a big ruby kiss imprint on the mirror.

I got the pearls. I couldn't put those on myself so I went into the kitchen. Kim came in wearing the silver rhinestone halter.

"You have lipstick on your teeth," Kim said. She handed me a piece of a paper towel. I used her dress as a mirror to clean my teeth and I adjusted the wig.

"Dang," I said. "How does anyone, male or female, manage it all? You're gonna have to put this necklace on me." I handed her the string of pearls and she helped me get them around my neck and clasped them.

"Yeah, lucky for us it's a one-time deal," Kim said.

"Oh, you delicate flower!" I said to Kim, trying to put my loud, low voice up an octave.

"You sugar 'n' spice, beauty shop bimbo!" she said.

"You thong-lovin' domestic goddess."

"You Maybelline mascara lush!" she said. We

laughed. I showed Kim my leg, with the suntan pantyhose. "What do you think looks better? The suntan hose or the fishnets?"

"Have you lost your mind?" Kim said. "June Cleaver never wore fishnets! She didn't even know what fishnets were."

"I dunno. Maybe she was all into S&M with Ward." I held up my purse, yeah, like I said, I had a purse, it was Chad's too. I had never owned a purse before, and I didn't see a lot of purses in my future. "I got wire cutters in here and some plastic bags for the money. Is Baby ready on Hermann?"

"Yeah," Kim said, "and finding a spot there with the parade was not easy!"

"Spare key?" I asked.

"I'll drive," Kim said.

"I need a key!" I said.

"I'm driving the getaway Scion!" Kim said.

"But there's no guarantee who'll get to Baby first. We can't risk it."

Kim knew I was right. She opened the fridge. Our fridge was divided by painter's blue tape down the center, one side was mine, one side Kim's. It really didn't stop me from eating her food. Kim opened a loaf of bread. In between slices, there was a spare key. I looked at it. All the places I had looked and that's where it had been hidden.

"If anything happens to her, you're dead!" Kim said. "You know, we still don't have a plan."

"Trust me. It's all gonna work out. I have a feeling." It all just sounded hollow, even to me. "I guess this is where we depend on the feminine. Creativity. Intuition. Bitching."

"Where's Chad?" Kim asked.

"He'll be here in a minute. I left the door open for him. You know what, your butt looks pretty delicious in that mirrored-ball dress. I wouldn't have guessed it."

I was checking out Kim's butt and she was trying to look at it too, and we heard Chad coming down the steps. "There he is," I said.

Then Lynne walked in through the open door. "Are you leaving for the – " She looked at us with a look of pure confusion. "What?" she said. "What is this?" Lynne looked from me to Kim. Then Chad walked in wearing his butterfly costume.

Chad came in and he was spinning around. He didn't see Lynne. "C'mon girls! Time to grab that money fresh off the presses!"

"What?" Lynne said. "What money?"

Chad stopped spinning and put his hands on his hips, his rainbow wings behind him. He was miffed. "Oh, so that's how it is!" he said. "You said you weren't going to tell her we were robbing the Mint!" And that was all it took. Chad had spilled the beans to Lynne, and he didn't even realize he did it.

"Robbing the Mint? Are you crazy? They'll kill you!! All my coaching! You're not doing that. I'm calling the police."

"That's exactly what I'd expect from a... a... friend like you!" I said. Crazy, yes. Not doing that, maybe. But police – no.

Lynne turned and she started to leave. I grabbed her, then Kim got another arm. Chad had no idea what was going on, but he grabbed her too.

"Get something!" I yelled.

Kim grabbed a pair of panty hose that was tossed on one of the kitchen chairs. We tied Lynne to the chair with a couple of pairs of panty hose and we gagged her with a small silk scarf. We made sure she could breathe and all.

I sort of dusted my hands off. I nodded my head to the panty hose. "I knew that girl crap would be good for something." Lynne struggled a bit. "One of us will untie you later." I turned on the TV. "Don't struggle," I said. "Here, you can watch the parade on TV." We positioned the chair so she could see the TV. It wasn't terrible, and it wasn't like she would be tied up forever.

Well, Lynne's appearance had been an unexpected delay, or maybe just a complete shock, but it was over and we were headed out the door. I hoped nothing else would go wrong. Kim and I stepped out the door with Chad behind us and he froze. He grabbed on to the door frame. I really think I heard his fingernails gouging into the wood. Now this was an issue I should have anticipated. All Chad did was live and breathe drag, talk about it incessantly, parade around the house in a complete whorehouse of outfits, but he had never worn a single rhinestone outside. I should have realized there would be an issue. Kim and I looked at each other. We both started coming up with a way to trick Chad out of the house. I thought about tossing a quarter down the steps, so he would cross the threshold and at least be out, but Chad didn't want a quarter. "Come on, all your friends are waiting!" I said. "The float needs you!" It was my pathetic voice, and we all knew my pleas weren't going to work.

Chad was breathing heavily. He finally spoke and said each word with a complete breath. "I. Can't.

Do. It."

"Sure, you can!" I said, and I didn't know what else to say, so I just kept saying it over and over again. "Sure, you can! Sure, you can!" It was the most unconvincing pleading you'd ever heard.

"It's okay," Kim said. "You don't need to go. I talked to the queen in charge of the float and she said she got some butterfly wings like you, so it's taken care of."

"She WHAT?" Chad said and he burst down the steps. "I'm gonna kill that bitch! Steal my idea! Copy my outfit! I'll kill her!" Chad raced down the stairs and was marching down the street. It was hard for us to keep up. After nearly a block, Chad said, "Kim, I never gave you Lisa's number."

"I'll explain on the way," Kim said. Kim was smart as shit, but she had always used her brilliance for good instead of evil. I could feel the wire cutters in the purse with every step. We were on our way!

Chapter 18 – I Love A Parade

And before we knew it, and with minimal complaining, we were at the parade and if you haven't been there, let me try and explain. Let's say you were an anime character, or maybe even better, you're Hello Kitty, or something like that. And you dropped acid. And all of a sudden, the world transformed into colors and rainbows, people wearing balloons for clothes, bare-chested men with perfect bodies, banners, and flags, and women riding motorcycles, a kaleidoscope of craziness and somehow, it all makes sense and it's all good.

The parade participants and gawking crowd synthesized into a beautiful freakfest. Chad, dressed in his butterfly drag, raced to the float. Kim and I were slower. I wore the kitten heels, and I would be damn glad when I had my sneakers back on. The float was done up in rainbow colors and had large letters that read "EMBRACE YOUR FABULOSITY!" On the back it said, "Out 4 Justice." Oh, and there were dance poles. You heard me right. Stripper poles. For dancing.

Chad ran up to the float and called up to the other drag queens. "Girls, girls! Here I am!" He opened his wings. The other drag queens seemed to be a bit jealous, but they lifted him up and onto the float. Kim and I watched from the street as Chad flaunted his outfit, fluttering his wings and strutting up and down the float. It was hard to imagine this was his first time in drag in public. "So whaddya think?" he asked.

"Huh! My sanitary pad has bigger wings!" said a drag queen who I later found out was Lisa Box. She had on a wig that was almost two feet high. She was a white girl, and her wig was hella red, like a magenta color. It was a beehive, and it looked really nice, sort of like a magenta Marge Simpson look. She wore this gown made out of, I think it's called tulle. It was an incredible frock of cobalt blue and fuchsia tulle; it had a stunning V-neck and the colors of blue and fuchsia alternated and flowed behind her. And I can tell I'll never be a fashion reporter, because I can't describe how great these women looked, but whether you were male or female or intersex, or gay or straight, genderqueer, or something along the spectrum, one glance at these women gave your brain a hard-on and you could only stare at them, with open-mouthed imbecility.

"Oh Chad, you're a butter-flop. But on you it looks good," said the queen who turned out to be Amina Bitch.

Chad introduced us. "This is Lisa. Lisa Box."

Lisa Box said, "Lisa DeBris-Box. Of the DeBris-Boxes."

"And this is Amina. Amina Bitch."

Amina said, "Enchanté." There were five or six other queens on the float, and I figured we'd meet them later.

"These are the friends I told you about: Lotta Baggage and Coco Puffs," Chad said.

I was completely intimidated, and I could see Kim felt the same way. And then it dawned on me, Kim and I started out female and we were intimidated about being dressed like girls by two people that hadn't started life as biological females. Oh well. Hands down, the queens had won the femininity game, so I figured I should just shut up and try and learn from them.

Amina Bitch tapped her long red nails on her breasts. "Oh dearie, when they said 'drag,' they didn't mean your ass."

Lisa Box spoke. "You said they were gonna

pass!"

Amina laughed in a way I would describe as haughty. "They couldn't even pass a toke!"

"C'mon now! They're virgins!" Chad said.

"Last I heard, so are you." Lisa Box was sizing us up. "I don't want 'em on our float."

Oh gawd. I hadn't even considered this, the thought that they wouldn't let us on. If we didn't get on the float, that was it, this thing was over.

Then Amina Bitch spoke with absolute disdain. "They didn't even help with fundraising!" Nothing could be lower in this community than not helping with the fundraising. Wow, if there was one thing I didn't want to be, it was a fundraising squelcher.

Lisa nodded at my purse. "What's that?" she asked.

I was guessing that maybe she wanted me to make a donation and I reached for my back pocket, thinking I had a five in there, but then I realized I didn't have my jeans on. I kind of held the purse up and said, "Uh... it's my make-up bag."

"Well hon, open it up," Amina said. "And see if there's a plastic surgeon stuffed inside." Amina and Lisa laughed.

"The makeup bag worked," Lisa said. "They put on makeup and they look like old bags. These boys really didn't try very hard."

Kim and I looked at each other and I said to her softly, "Run!"

"They're my friends, and they're coming with us!" Chad said. And that was that. Someone defended me for the first time in my life. A few of the drag queens grabbed Kim and pulled her onto the float. Then they grabbed me by the arms and lifted me up. As I rose in the air, I saw the banner of the float behind us. It was a huge banner of flowers that read: "You Are a Child of the Universe!"

"It's a world of freaks and I'm a... a freak," I said. "Kim, I AM a part of the universe. I am! Even me!"

Kim nodded to the freaks on the You Are a Child of the Universe float. "I don't think you wanna be a part of that universe."

My line of sight moved from the banner to the float participants. They were gay men dressed as babies, in diapers and stuff. One was in a playpen. Two were being spanked. Ick. Definitely not my thing. Like I said, I'm for everything, but that doesn't mean I'm strapping on a diaper.

Lisa Box came over and inspected me. She didn't

say a word, just gave looks of disapproval. I felt myself make a fist, ready to clock Lisa in the head. Kim saw and grabbed me by the forearm.

Kim whispered to me, "Don't lose it."

I released my fist and contained myself, maybe for the first time ever! Lisa stood next to me; she had to be a foot taller than me, then had the two-foot wig on top. She pointed out the other drag queens. "This is Kitty Litter, Betty Will, Rolanda Joint, and Sharon D. Henny."

Chad fluttered over on his tall silver spikes. "Don't forget me: Carmen Gettit!!!" Then he fluttered away.

The queens were all definitely Embracing their Fabulosity. Kitty Litter was a big girl. She wore a huge blue wig that curled at the bottom. She had painted on some pouty crimson lips and had perfectly curved eyebrows that rose up on her face like the St. Louis arch. She wore glittery pink eyeshadow, embellished with a black outline. The huge eyebrows went up to the top of her hairline. She blinked her eyelashes and they must have been two inches long. She wore silky gloves that traveled up above her elbow. She had on an outfit covered with pink and blue bubbles made out of plastic, and she capped off the look with a hat with a cluster of tiny pink and blue bubbles.

Sharon D. Henny wore a fluorescent orange bustier and a tight orange skirt, but I guessed those hips had to be padded because she had an unbelievable hourglass figure. She had an orange wig that rolled down her shoulders and curled up on her bosom like a sleeping pup. She wore what I would describe as a feather stole – it wrapped around her shoulders. Long feathers, mostly orange and blue, aimed down, ready for flight, and the feathers on top rose around her like the collar on the Evil Queen from Snow White. It was crazy good.

The bustier was tight and she looked hot. She had on silver nails, sharpened like cat claws. It looked like she had put on each false eyelash separately. Her boobs looked real. I wasn't sure. Did she have on some sort of prosthetic? Had she pushed her pecs into that bustier in a voluptuous way? Or maybe she was taking hormones and had started growing some... I couldn't tell. She had on huge, costume jewelry bracelets, giant fake diamonds that were blinding when they caught a glint of sun. Betty Will had on a crazy geometric dress made from iridescent fabric. Rolanda Joint was in red sequins and had a little red sequined top hat that I liked.

Everybody was splashes of rhinestones, sequins, feather, tulle, and fluff, and everyone's outfit made the Miss Universe Contest look like a kindergarten Halloween parade. I felt like an idiot, as I was no match for these beauties. This was like every day of my life. I was never going to fit in, but I reminded myself – means to an end. Today was about getting enough money to change my life, not whine about being an outsider. Right when I was rationalizing, I saw her. The most beautiful woman in the world. She was small, like me, Chinese, and she wore an outfit from the sixties, white go-go boots, and a vinyl black and white checkered mini-dress. She had a black and white cap that she had jauntily tugged to the side. She wore the bright red lipstick, everyone's favorite, apparently, and she had a black bob. She walked over to me.

"Introduce yourself!" Lisa Box yelled at me.

"I'm Lotta Baggage," I said.

She extended her hand to me and said, "Olive Yu."

"I love you, too," I said, and everyone laughed. Luckily, people thought I was being funny when I was really just an idiot.

The float had a huge sound system and all the drag queens on the float were dancing to the music. I would love to tell you their moves were suggestive, but that could not capture the sluttiness, the crudeness, the sheer depravity of their dancing. I loved watching it, but there was no way I could do it. Kim and I leaned against the float letters that spell out FABULOSITY! Lisa stared at us.

"You gonna shake that money maker, girlfriend, or just sit on it?"

"Technically," I said, "I'm standing." This was not the right answer.

We both started to move. Kim did her best, but she was terrible. Her dance was sort of the running man and sort of not. About all I could do was the "White Man's Overbite." Here we were struggling to stay up, wiggling around on the heels, while the other drag queens on the float made "Girls Gone Wild" look like an episode of "Gumby." Some straight guy walked up to the float. He was drinking a beer from a bag.

He looked at me and said, "Nice ass."

I couldn't believe that this stupid straight boy said this to me! I walked over to the side of the float and punched him, solid in the jaw. The other drag queens on the float all looked at me in shock. Chad rushed over. The straight guy staggered away.

Lisa Box walked over and stood there with her giant red lips. She crossed her arms and tapped her nails on one elbow. "He just complimented you and you hit him. What are you thinking?"

I looked at Kim. Was our whole world turned upside down?

"Sorry," I said. "I have a mild to moderate case of Tourette's." I punched my arm in the air a few times, pretending the punch was involuntary.

Lisa Box blinked her giant eyelashes at me. I had never thought that someone could make a statement just by blinking her eyes, but she had done it. The reprimand continued. "You're a drag queen, honey. If they want some of this..." and Lisa box grabbed my boobs. "Or this," she grabbed my ass. My mouth was wide open. This was the most action I'd had all year.

"When they want some of that, the correct response is 'Thank you sir, again, please.'"

I said, "Uh...what about 'no means no?'"

Chad rolled his eyes and gave me a look that said 'don't act crazy.'

Lisa Box had no clue where I was coming from. She said, "No means no... stopping!" She grabbed my boobs again and was squishing them. "Hey, what are you using? It's good. It's not bird seed."

"Uh...foam." I couldn't believe I was getting

manhandled. Or womanhandled. It was all crazy. I had to remember. Means to an end.

Lisa Box said, "Well, neither of you pass. But I'll let you fail under my watchful eye. Good thing you're only a virgin once."

"Sorry," I said. "I won't hit anyone else. It was just a shock."

Lisa Box said, "I can understand that. With that ass, it's a shock anyone was interested!" Lisa tossed her fiery red hair back. The wig wiggled like a tower of cherry jello then stabilized. Lisa moved to a different part of the float.

What had just happened? I just stood there stunned. I hadn't felt this way since the seventh grade when I first got boobs and the boys were always grabbing them and you had to fight them all off. How many years had I spent yelling at guys, telling them to keep their hands off me? I knew drag queens didn't just let people touch them. This all had to be for the parade.

Chad walked over to me and Kim was there. He said, "Look, to make this work, you've got to –"

Kim cut him off. "Apply some empathy?"

"Hide?" I said.

Chad gave us a look. "I was gonna say: be a slut. I know you have no experience, just try and fake it, so I don't get kicked off too."

So I stood there contemplating what the fuck I had gotten myself – and Kim – into. I was a sorry excuse for a female. And this was the best I could do, slathering on eye shadow, clipping in fake hair, and stuffing my grabbable ass into Chad's clothes.

And after standing around for more than an hour, the float finally took off. It really caught me off guard and I almost fell. I had to grab onto a rail. The speakers blared Fergie's "Glamorous." Kim was waving the queen's wave, and I could see she was looking for me, but I was climbing off the back of the float. Kim saw me and came running. She was a little unsteady on the heels.

"Where are you going?" she said in a pretty unpleasant tone.

"I can't do this!" I said. "I can't do what I've rebelled against for almost four decades! Wearing a dress and fashion and boob-grabbing and pretending I like people looking at me. I can't do it! I quit!"

"What?" Kim said. "You dragged me into this! And now you're gonna quit? I got an idea. Why don't you just go fuck your–"

Chad strutted over. He gave us his look of disapproval.

Kim said, "Why don't you just go… embrace your fabulosity!"

"Good idea!" Chad said. I couldn't even say Chad had A.D.D. because people with A.D.D. had a much longer attention span than Chad. He couldn't stay mad at you because he couldn't remember to stay mad at you. I climbed back onto the float. It felt like my wig was a little crooked, but what was I going to do?

"Come on girls!" Chad said. "Work that Fabulosity! Watch me!" Chad headed for the pole.

"You gotta do this!" Kim said. "You gotta win. For me. For gays everywhere. For every fuck-up that ever lived."

"No plan. No skills. No diversion," I said.

"Even if we don't succeed, we gotta go for it. We gotta try," Kim said. "Plus, I wore a dress! I may as well get some use out of it."

"All right. All right I'll try," I said.

"Think of one of your skills," Kim said. "If you're good at one thing, you can be good at all things."

"That makes no sense at all," I said.

"What are you good at?" Kim asked.

"Hmm," I said. There wasn't much to choose from.

"C'mon! You gotta have some kind of success!" Kim said.

"I pack a mean tub of the Colonel's coleslaw," I said.

"Then we can do this! Just transfer that skill!"

"I don't get it," I said.

"Feel the way you feel about packing the coleslaw, then dance. And you'll be good at it." I wasn't convinced. I was sliding my hand across the pearls, from bead to bead to bead. "Those pearls? Those pearls make you a winner."

"Yeah. They do," I said.

"Good," Kim said. "Now, shake that ass!"

Chad was wiggling his ass and everything else and the crowd was going berserk. He flaunted what he had on the catwalk, then held a rail and swung his head around and around. Then he sort of did a backbend and kicked his leg up high. The crowd went crazy. He must not have been wearing any underpants.

Kim looked at me and shrugged. Kim strutted, well more or less, then joined Chad's dance. Kim slapped Chad's ass like he was a naughty pony. The crowd loved it. Chad waved me over. This was the point when I realized I was actually very shy and for all my progressiveness and post-liberalism, when it came to my own body, I was a prude. I would be better off dressed like an old Amish lady with a dress that covered every speck of skin and buttoned up to my chin.

Chad came over and grabbed me by the arm and started dragging me to the pole. "No, dude," I said. "I'm. Not. Dancing. On a pole. A freaking pole!" And I couldn't stop him, he was bigger than me and he dragged me to the pole. I know the wig was now starting to come undone, a string of hair fell into my eyes. "I'm not gonna do it!" I said in fear.

Kim looked at me then said, "You said you'd do anything."

I had said that hadn't I? Why had I said that? I looked at the crowd. What was I doing here? I could have put on the brakes yesterday. Gone to the parade with Daneetra. Spent the rest of my life busting my hump at KFC. Grown into a bitter, but slightly satisfied, old lady. But I hadn't put on the brakes. And I was standing on a float in a freaking dress in front of only three-quarters of a million people. I was here. I had chosen to do this. Well, then dammit, I was gonna do it. I committed. I took a deep breath and did my best to invoke the spirit of Barbara Billingsley. All the other queens had on provocative, trampy outfits, but mine was actually quite innocent. The fifties look, the fresh-pressed linen, the fabric actually felt special, like someone cared, like maybe if my mom had lived, maybe she would have worn a dress like this. I marched down that float, I displayed the skirt to the crowd, like a curtsy without the bend and suddenly, the crowd was cheering for me. They didn't just love the whorey queens, they liked the fifties mom, too. I fingered the pearls and with one finger I displayed them to the crowd. The crowd loved that too. This crowd loved me being a female faking a male who was imitating a girl. And right then the whole world made as much sense to me as it ever would. And all of a sudden, I thought of the kid singing karaoke at the Mint. Whether it was an audience of one or one million, he gave it everything. And today, this was the one million audience show. I looked over and saw Chad was slowing humping the pole. It wasn't exactly what I would call dancing, but what the hell? I decided to go for it.

I slid up to the pole, ready to give it my best shot. Should I be a slutty Mrs. Cleaver, slowly thrusting her hips against the pole? Should I try and climb the pole? If only I had a tray of cupcakes to display to this ravenous, horndog crowd! First, I spun around the pole and the skirt twirled up in the air, sort of like Marilyn Monroe in that movie. The crowd was going crazy. I leaned back against the pole and slowly lifted my leg in the air. I got some serious cat calls with that. Chad was miffed. What dances did I know? The Macarena? The Cha Cha Slide? This was all too pathetic. Then I remembered my babysitter had taught me a compilation of dances from the fifties and sixties. I did The Twist, The Swim, and a little of The Bat Dance. Then all of a sudden, I recalled some of the stuff the kids from the bakery had taught me how to do, something they called booty popping. It's what we now call twerking. Not sure why I had to be so reflective in the middle of absolute chaos, but for all my bitching at Chad about cultural appropriation, if I did that dance, this would be the worst cultural appropriation ever! A million times worse than Chad. Except this was different. I was trying to save my ass. Damn, I was justifying what I was doing. That was a sure sign of cultural appropriation. Well, I thought, fuck me. I don't know what else to do. Twerking it was.

I held on to the pole and I shook my ass. First, I just wiggled my knees to make my butt dance. It was pretty good! Most people in this crowd hadn't seen that kind of move. When we had a lull, some of the bakery workers had shown me all kinds of moves. I remembered some of the names, the bounce, the bend over, the wild wood, booty clapping. I went into a squat and popped my butt out, moving my hips quickly. Then I bent over and grabbed onto the pole. I made sure the crowd had a side view so they could see what I was doing. I hoisted my hiney up as high as I could get it. There's was the smallest gust of wind ever and the skirt flew up and covered my head. So much for being shy. Luckily, I had put some clean white panties on over the panty hose. I stayed bent over and kept my balance by holding on the pole and I was jiggling that jelly for all it was worth. Let's be real. I had chubby, unformed buns, and I was a rhythmless white queer girl, so my ass shaking wasn't perfect, but it was definitely a crowd pleaser. I stood up, still held on to the pole and ended with a full on twerk, I shook my knees and my ass cheeks slapped like a twenty-pound uncured ham. People went nuts. I knew I had done Mrs. Cleaver proud.

Finally, I stopped to catch my breath. Kim just stood there with a look that asked 'do I know you?'

"Well! Miss Thang!" Chad said.

Lisa Box walked over and lifted that brow. She pursed her huge, ruby lips. She lifted that judgmental brow. "Kudos to me!" she said. "I've done it again."

Chapter 19 – Minty-Fresh

I had done my duty. I had paid my dues as a drag queen on the float. Now I had to get back to business. We were on Market near 8th Street. We were heading for the end of the line. I needed to make a move. Kim looked at me.

"What now?" Kim asked.

"I dunno," I said. "Trust me. I'll think of something. I won't steer ya wrong." Steer! That was it! I moved to the front of the float and I held on tight as I leaned over and shoved my mug through the window to talk to the driver of the float. When I stuck my head in the driver's side window, I saw the float driver was also in drag, wearing a scarlet red rhinestone gown. It must have been a drag – heh – so to speak – to drive in the dress.

"Who are you?" I asked.

"I'm Minnie," she said. Then she nodded toward her crotch. "Though trust me, it's not."

"Lemme guess," I said. "Minnie Driver?"

"Minnie Cooper," she said.

I slapped the driver side door. "Lemme drive," I said.

"Forget it sister! Nothing's getting me from behind this wheel!" I grabbed her sleeve and tried to drag her out. "What's your trip?" she said.

"I just wanted to give you a break. Hey, there's tequila shots up on the float," I said.

"I'm clean and sober," she said. Wasn't that just great, I thought. Every other person in this City chugged alcohol like it was oxygen and I had to run into the rare clean and sober gay. I tried to think of something else that could lure her out.

"You should see these girls dance on the pole!" I said.

"I've seen it," she said. "I choreographed it." Of course, you did, I thought.

"Did you know there's a safe glory hole off the starboard bow. I wanted you to get a chance to – ." Minnie was gone before I could even finish the sentence. I climbed behind the wheel. This was some kind of old American car, like maybe a Belvedere with a three on the tree. I hadn't driven a shit bucket like this in decades. I floored it. The massive float was tearing up the road at about seven miles per hour. There was a little video camera that let me see what was happening on the float. With the added acceleration, two queens slipped and grabbed each other.

I could feel my pulse increase as I made the choice. I felt my blood pressure shift. It was happening. I went off course. Instead of taking the turn near Civic Center, I crashed through the yellow caution tape and the little orange pylons. That was all that was stopping me, caution tape and construction pylons. I could see the parade monitors going nuts, waving their clipboards, flapping their arms. What were they going to do? This American made monster weighed tons. They couldn't stop me. This thing was like a battleship, like the Titanic – no, not the Titanic! I tried to wipe that image out of my head. I could hear my breathing at this point, and I could see the queens were trying to figure out what was going on. They knew where the parade ended and surely they wanted to hit the Civic Center and start partying. In the little camera I could see Chad and Kim trying to brush it off, like it was no big deal, calming people so it wouldn't turn into a panic.

All of a sudden, Lisa Box stuck her head in the window. "Minnie! End of the line! I need to refill the margaritas!" Lisa was so close I could feel the light sweep of her lashes as she blinked trying to put two and two together.

"Minnie went AWOL," I said. "Don't worry. I'll get us home." Lisa disappeared. Then I noticed something I hadn't planned on, and since I hadn't planned anything, this was par for the course. The float behind us had followed us. It didn't turn, it didn't take the turn near Civic Center to go park the float and begin partying, no, it played follow-the-leader and was behind me. And the float behind them followed them and all of a sudden, I could see five or six more floats behind me. I pushed the accelerator all the way to the floor and got it up to eight miles an hour. Since I was now off the parade route, I was hitting traffic. I plowed through the slow line of cars, like a big gay tank. That Mint was so close I could taste it!

I made a right on Buchanan; it's a pretty steep grade, and I could hear the engine groaning like an old man having a bad dream. I shifted to first and crept up the hill. Then I made a left on Hermann and what happened next was pure synchronicity. A truck was coming out of the Mint, using the smaller drive. It was Sunday. It was Pride week. What on earth was so important it needed to be delivered on a Sunday? Or could it be an employee leaving? But as the truck drove out, the black fence had rolled open and though the float was slow, the timing seemed perfect. As soon as the truck exited, I would pull in while the gate was still open. The truck pulled away, but the float was so slow, the gate closed. I kept going and smashed the little black rails to smithereens. Nothing was going to stop this beast. Again, this hadn't been on my "to-do" list, but I had plowed through fencing. I rolled up the concrete and prepared to park, but I don't know what happened; I really think I hit the brakes, but for whatever reason, nothing stopped and I rammed the monster right into the building. No damage was done to that concrete slab, but a couple of queens jumped off to save their necks. I got out to surmise the damage. The float was shredded and collapsed. The music track was starting over and "Glamorous" started blaring again from the speakers, but within a minute the voice keeled over, bleated, and died.

The guard from the cop box came running over to investigate. The float was in pretty sorry shape. The front was demolished and luckily there had been enough front crumple space from the float that I survived to describe it. The banner that read EMBRACE YOUR FABULOSITY was torn to hell and had been reduced to BE FABU. Lisa Box was near tears. "Oh no!" she said. "Our float is ruined!"

Amina Bitch observed, "Fabu survived."

Immediately Lisa Box was jubilant. "Then that's

our new motto – BE FABU! Forge ahead, girls! A new venue! Be Fabu! Fabu!"

I was totally cool after the crash, but I needed to get into the building and the door was right in front of me, wide open. I just needed to walk in, fill up my bags with money, then treat myself to a nice lunch. Right when I had that thought, I heard a crash. I looked east. The float that was behind us had crashed through the larger gate and I watched as it rolled up the drive and it crashed into the side of the building. Damn! Couldn't they think of anything original? Another float followed them, chugged over the smashed gate, and parked, politely, in the drive. The riders on those floats headed for the building. It took me a minute before I realized they thought this was one of the parade's venues. By then, another float had driven in and crashed into the other float. Every minute or so, another float would "crash" the party, so to speak.

I needed to act, but I just spaced out. I started imagining what would happen once we got in. I could see the drag queens from our float strutting into the main work floor. Two more guards had joined the cop in the box and they looked like they wanted to grab the drag queens but were reluctant. Was it because they didn't want to touch the queens, or they didn't want a snarky morning Chronicle headline? Chad fluttered in.

Chad raised his wings to one of the guards. He said, "If you think these wings are something, you should see my chrysalis!"

The guards just stood there. Again, I wasn't sure if they were confused or scared, or repelled. For once, I thought, homophobia was working in my favor.

That's when one of the guards yelled, "Stop, or I'll shoot!"

Kitty Litter stroked the guard's chin and said, "Oh, I hope so. We could use some excitement."

Betty Will said, "Kill a queen, go to jail."

The guard yelled, "I said I'll shoot!"

Sharon D. Henny said, "Lemme pop a Viagra and we can shoot together!"

The guard said, "I'll use this baton!"

Sharon D. Henny liked this. "Ya will?" she said. "Terrific. Meet me in the bathroom in five. And bring some lube!"

A guard stood near the wall; I wasn't sure if it was the one Sharon D. Henny had propositioned. He called on his radio. "Thunderstorm the main floor," he said.

Whoever was on the other end said. "You can't

drop tear gas on this crowd!"

"Why not?" said the guard.

"Tear gas a buncha queens on gay parade day? That's a PR nightmare."

Lisa Box paraded around. "A new venue, girls!" Lisa saw the printing presses churning out money and shouted "Oh, we're in money heaven! Let's all do what the bills - circulate! Circulate!"

Sharon D. Henny went up to the guard she liked and asked, "Where can I get a martini?"

The guard was pissed. "We don't have any alcohol in here!"

Sharon D. Henny said, "Good thing I brought my own." She took a martini shaker and two glasses from her purse and started making some martinis. She said to the guard, "You look like an olive man. Me, I like a twist."

Another float crashed into the pile of floats and it snapped me out of my little fantasy. I don't know why, but I needed to be taking action and instead I was lost in a little reverie, making up scenes in my head, when I needed to be worried about real life.

By this time, there were four guards and they were trying to figure out what to do. Several hundred paradegoers had gathered in the drive of the Mint, most of them in costume, but some spectators. One of the floats had a DJ with major equipment and people pushed that float with the DJ in the smack center of the building and that's when the dance party started. "All right, all right, San Francisco! Why are we here?" the DJ screamed. "To party!" the crowd responded. "That's right! Happy Pride! We're gonna party all night!"

This crowd included drag queens, drag kings, trannies, gay parents pushing their strollers, PFLAGS (that's Parent, Families and Friends of Lesbians and Gays), the gay contingent from Google, those guys wearing the diapers, a two-spirits group, you know, basically another day at the office. While I was evaluating the terrain, SF Cheer, the cheerleading group, crashed their float, the San Francisco Lesbian/Gay Freedom Band marched in, and so did a group of leather daddies. Also, and I don't know how they made it up that hill without having a heart attack, but there was a group on roller skates waving gay flags. The DJ's music was blasting, then a float with a wedding arch rolled in and parked itself right by the DJ booth. On the float two women were getting married – the officiant looked like Elvis Herselvis. There was a group of gays with disabilities, so there were a few people using wheelchairs, a mobility scooter, a group of deaf gays, and some blind queers. A few dykes on bikes had driven in, and they were revving their cycles up, but at this point they couldn't get through the crowd. I saw one of the Sisters of Perpetual Indulgence, I think it was Sister Boom Boom.

It had been a few people, then a few hundred, and all of a sudden, it was really getting crowded. I could smell herb being passed around. Oh and, there was a little booze. And by a little booze, I mean a shitload of booze. I'm not sure if people had it in the first place or if someone had made a Safeway run, but this scene was starting to make a frat beer bust look like a kindergartener's birthday party.

I was standing there, looking at the flood of queens. Drag queens, drag kings, dykes, trannies, genderqueer, queers of all kinds, and all sorts of other fellow freaks. And I loved them all, though given my germaphobia, it was purely platonic. The entire fluidity of the sexual spectrum had arrived to help me. Tears rolled down my cheeks, causing my mascara to smear. Just as I had sworn I wouldn't do, there I was, crying in a dress, instead of kicking ass.

Kim walked up to me. I had lost track of her. "Are you crying?" she asked.

"No. I've got something in both my eyes."

"What?" Kim asked.

"My sorry-ass past," I said.

The guy who I think was the head guard held a hand up to the other guard, to hold his fire, I guess. You know, in certain situations in this country we would have been shot dead. But this was Pride Week. In San Francisco. You can't go around shooting drag queens. This would be the worst PR on the planet. That was when I realized it might have been easier just to buy a high-end printer and make some Funny Money. Breaking into the Mint seemed like an awful lot of trouble and I could have just been a counterfeiter. This was a lousy time for this realization.

I think I was in shock because I was looking around and realized the guards were gone and the front door was shut. Damn! What had I done? I needed to get in. I started yelling, "The real party's inside!" and no one heard me over the DJ. I climbed up on the DJ's float. "I've got a request," I yelled at him. Wow, at this point, the entire drive in front of the Mint was crammed with tons of people. I would guess two or three thousand people, but there was no way to tell. That's when I noticed the entrance door was closed. I grabbed the mic out of the DJ's hand. "Everyone! The real party is inside! We have to get inside." I may as well have been asking a scurry of squirrels to build the Golden Gate Bridge.

Everything was out of control. All this beautiful gay life force, if only there was some way I could harness the insanity for my own gain. People were just jumping around and dancing, and everyone was having the good time they had come for. Was there any way to organize a giant pile of partying gays? There was only one way. I took a deep breath, then another, then I pulled the trigger. I whispered my request into the DJ's ear. He nodded and programmed the song. "Come on party people! The party is inside! Let's get in there!"

And then the song blasted out, in all its beauty. The DJ played "Gonna Make You Sweat." You hear that title and you think you don't know that song, but yes. Yes, you do know that song, but you know it as "Everybody Dance Now." And in your little head right now, you can sing that title in your bouncing gray matter falsetto. Everybody Dance Now. It was one of those gay anthems that no matter what you were doing, you would hear the mean bomp-bomp-bomp-bomp-bomp of the bass followed by that line, Everybody Dance Now. While there were other words in the song, no one knew any of them, and no one needed to know any of them. They only needed the primal thump that commanded Everybody Dance Now, and that sound bomp-bomp-bomp would trip a Pavlovian response. And of course, with this crowd, that's exactly what it did. Everyone started to dance.

Every freaky deaky dance style was accepted and embraced. If I had thought things were out of control before, they were just getting started.

It was almost robotic at first. Everyone responded to the beat, then the energy in the air, the alcohol, the music, whatever it was, made the crazed crowd decide it needed to get into the building, just as I had asked. Maybe the first thing that happened was somebody took a gay flag and smashed the tip through one of the lower windows. I knew I had asked for this, but when it was actually happening, I got a little worried. People were shoving on the door, but there was no way that thing was opening. Then a group started pulling at the base of our float and they tore a chunk of it off. I don't know if it was wood or metal, but it was a rectangular object, more or less. They started using it as a battering ram on one of the low windows, but they just didn't have the manpower. They were also trying to ram it to the beat of the music and that wasn't a great idea. That's when one of the dykes on bikes came up from the rear and helped shove the battering ram. With that extra power from the motorcycle, the battering ram demolished the metal bars and the window. The team used the battering ram to clear the glass and they climbed in. Someone tied a rope, or something like it, on the bars on the next window and the dyke on the bike took off and tore it away. Someone else smashed and cleared the glass and more people climbed in. The crowd was going wild, screaming and dancing, though I think they were just celebrating, not being excited that the windows were broken. In under a minute the people that had climbed in threw the door open and the partygoers stormed the building. Remember, I like to keep count of things, but I really couldn't now. I could only guess there were maybe two or three thousand people in the front drive and they were now all pushing through the entry. I jumped in the middle of the crowd. Kim saw me and wiggled her way to my side.

We were pushing our way in, and it was packed, but I could hear one of the guards screaming on his radio. "Goddamn Parade!" he said. "We need backup. I know every SFPD is covering the parade! Yes! No! This IS the parade! I AM in the Mint!" Right when he was saying that, he got a mouthful of fuchsia boa feathers. The guard spat them out. "I just got a boa in my mouth. A boa! Not a boa constrictor! Just send help!" And like that, somehow, it had worked. We were in.

We went through another door, then there was a metal detector everyone ignored. The music was still nice and loud even though we were inside, and this was actually the type of venue that could have served as an outstanding underground club, so people were starting to make the most of it. We walked into the lobby, and for all the cold, stern, plain-Jane looks of the outside, the inside rocked. First, there was an inlaid marble floor that included an eight-star compass. The arms of the star were brass with an etched design, and the center looked serpentine. It was a beautiful, polished disc of loveliness. I couldn't enjoy it as much as I would have liked to because so many people had crammed into the room. Straight ahead was a giant, and I mean giant, gold door. It was the size of a door and half, or maybe even two doors! I noticed the ceiling was also gold, and I don't think it was gold spray paint. I was thinking it might be real gold.

There were two elevators, I think they were elevators, on each side of the giant door. I didn't think the elevators were a good idea for us, so we'd have to use the steps behind us. This place looked huge on the outside, but it wasn't so big on the inside. People were already gathering on those steps and we needed to look casual while we got moving. The rest of the room had a bunch of plaques, some oversized coins glued to the wall, and a big marble eagle. I was planning our exit up the steps when the Freedom Band fired up and started playing, "San Francisco," but not the one about flowers in your hair; it was the one about opening your Golden Gate. Well, of course SF Cheer had a routine that went with it, so there's this goddamn marching band, with the trombones and the glockenspiels that were splitting my eardrum, and there was SF Cheer doing a freaking basket toss of a femmy queer girls. Then the boys would high kick and scream and giggle. That was when one of the dykes on bikes drove her motorcycle up the steps. This is all while the DJ is still blasting music, which of course had to be "YMCA" right then. It was the urban chaos that I both dreaded and longed for. I looked at Kim and used my head to motion to the steps.

We tried to walk up the stairs nonchalantly, and given the fact that the stairs were full of gay cheerleaders, I thought we were pretty successful. The stairs were pretty nondescript, though they had some nice brass railings that some poor stooge probably had to polish all day. Luckily, it was day and the lights were on, so it was easy for me to wander around. If we ran into a guard, I would just say we were looking for a bathroom, a gender neutral one.

The first room we went into had a long, wide table with stacks of white towels. I wasn't sure what that was at all. I saw bags – I looked inside and they were full of slugs, waiting to be turned into coins. I wasn't interested in the coins; I was looking for the paper money. But it was pretty cool to see the slugs.

There were thousands of them and they were super shiny. That's when I realized I'd lost the purse and it had the bags in it. But they were just garbage bags and those coins made me realize the garbage bags probably wouldn't be strong enough to hold the paper money. I guess that's why movies always had bank robbers take the money in canvas bags. Other parade participants were filling the room, and a couple of guys were making out and ending up lying on the towels. Ick. A few people were spinning around, tossing the slugs, and they bounced off the floor with a nice ring.

This place looked like a high-tech boiler room. There were lots of gray machines with thermostats. I wasn't sure what these were. At one point I found what looked like a giant barrel full of BBs. Then I found these round, plastic bins full of slugs, but these slugs had the ridged edge of a coin. I figured they were getting those ready to make quarters or something.

I split; Kim saw me and we both walked into another room. This place had a bunch of large, blue machines in it. I counted eighteen machines, but there may have been more. Well, what I wanted was to be grabbin' the money. The machine looked like a little blue coffee shack. I turned one on. The machine started spitting out coins that slid into a black tray.

The machine I was at was making quarters. They were so shiny! Like little round mirrors. I guessed the coins started out that glossy till they hit our dirty hands and got all cruddy. Anyhow, I had made it! I was in the place that made the money! Kim and I turned on all the blue machines and coins were rolling out. To me, each time a quarter got pressed and rolled out to the tray it sounded like ka-ching!

But I still needed to find the printing press.

I think we went up the stairs to the next floor, but I honestly don't remember. We went into a room and it was full of yellow robots. I counted thirteen then I turned them all on, hoping this was how the money was going to appear. They didn't look like printing presses, but maybe this was a new process. Conveyer belts clicked into action. A robotic arm started placing coins into a plastic coin case, then another robot added a different coin. When they were full, the coin cases were picked up by a yellow, robotic arm that stacked them into a cardboard box. The arms would pick up a filled box and carry it to a scale. The robots were fast – and they were sending the packs down a conveyer belt that went who knows where? There were endless stacks of these coin sets, but I didn't want something that was worth less than five bucks of change. I wanted the paper money. Kim picked up one of the plastic boxes. It had five quarters in it. "I don't want a dollar!" I said. And this was the world's least cost-effective packaging, putting five quarters in a plastic box. I started wondering how many guards were working Sunday. I thought I had seen five. Five guards and two thousand partying gays. We could take our time and find the printing press.

Chapter 20 – Money, Money, Money, Money

We weren't sure what to do, so we started to backtrack. We ended up back in the room with the blue machines that pressed coins. Where were the damn printing presses? The parade participants had taken over the Mint, turning the sterile factory into a happening party spot. I had left all the machines on and coins were pouring from the hopper making this seem like the ideal club. We could hear the music from the DJ outside and as we backtracked, we saw people dancing on the floor and on the machines. A buff guy wearing scanty leather shorts and working a boa strutted on one of the coin makers and another guy wearing only rainbow balloons was working his stuff nearby.

People just kept pouring in. I can't tell you how many queers had crammed into the place. This place may have been built for like a hundred people, but everyone was so used to being in crowded clubs, no one cared. A samba group threaded a conga line across the floor, a gay parents group pushed in the stroller brigade, and Clean and Sober Gays marched in carrying their banner.

At this point, it seemed every GiBLeT freak of the multicultural multigendered rainbow had strolled in for the party: leatherdaddies, leathergirls, disabled gays, transgendered, heavily tatted and pierced, senior gays, deaf, AIDS protestors, even the dudes in diapers, you name it. More Dykes on Bikes had joined. Though they had finished first, they had double backed to see what was up. They rode their cycles in and across the floor, popping wheelies and gunning their engines. It was just like every party in the City, somehow word got out and the place was jam-packed. There was booze all over the place. Somebody offered me a bottle of vodka, and I took a healthy swig.

I looked around. "I was in a casino in Reno just like this."

Kim said, "What a frikken mess!"

"This is no mess, friend," I said. "It's Situation Normal: All SF. Can you believe this? And I thought I couldn't do anything. You wanted a diversion?" I smiled and I held my arms open to show the beauty of my distraction. "It's absolutely perfect. You asked for a diversion and I deliver. My only regret is I may have to share some of the money."

"Okay, we gotta make this happen," Kim said. "Let's get Chad to help."

Chad, still in his butterfly suit, was spinning around in circles on top of a machine. Then he jumped on a bare-chested guy and rode him around like a pony.

I pointed at him. "See that? That's how Chad helps," I said.

Kim looked around. "Where should we start?"

"Macarena over there." We danced over to one of the machines that spat out the super shiny new coins.

Kim picked up a handful of the coins and let them pour from her hand back into the hopper. "Half a dollars," Kim said.

Of all the useless coins that exist, half dollars are up there on the list. But I didn't have the purse anymore and that had not only the wire cutters I didn't need, but also the bags I was going to use to carry the money. Though I had lost them, I knew those cheap plastic bags could only carry so many coins. At least I had put the spare Scion key in my bra.

I looked in another hopper. I was excited, I smiled, and I nodded my head. Kim reached in then confirmed.

"Half a dollars," she said.

We walked to a different bin. We had to dance with a few people on the way, but we finally reached the bin.

"What's the word?" Kim said.

"Half dollars," I said. "Keep going."

"Ben Franklins?" Kim asked.

"More half dollars," I said.

"Where's the printing press? Where's the paper money?" Kim asked.

"Let's try over there."

We walked to another machine, weaving our way through the crowd. We were hoisted up by the crowd and had to dance on the machines for a while. It was actually perfect because I could get the lay of the land. "Well, the view's better up here. Look!" I said. I looked down and inspected the machine I was on.

"Jackpot?" Kim asked.

"Half dollars," I said.

"Guess what?" Kim said.

"What?" I asked.

"I think this place only makes half a dollars," Kim said.

"Quite a brain you got there, Einstein," I said. "I'm gonna rent you out for private parties."

"We did all this for a bunch of half a dollars," Kim said. "Shit, we coulda just stole recycling. What do we do now?"

I stood there for a second. I didn't know what to do. Then I said, "They only got half dollars? We steal half dollars!"

I dove off the machine and into the mosh pit, followed by Kim. We were carried momentarily by the crowd. I hadn't crowd surfed in a long time. We landed and headed to the closest machine. Walking through the bedlam, I found a reusable grocery bag,

"Think you can carry 100 grand worth of half dollars?" I asked.

Kim showed her biceps. "With these guns?" she said. "Sure!"

We started loading up the half dollars, putting them everywhere we could stuff them. We were taking the loose coins which seemed like a better idea than the boxes, but I wasn't sure.

"Try and get enough to pay off my student loans," Kim said. She had stuffed lots of coins into her halter top and it was starting to sag.

"Let's go get some of those boxes of coins."

"Good idea," Kim said.

We went back to the robot room and the boxes were piled about three feet high and there were hundreds of piles. I was glad I'd snagged that grocery bag. We started stuffing boxes in our dresses, but we just didn't have enough room, boxes were falling on the floor. There were carts of these boxed coins and I wondered if we could just roll out a whole cart.

Kim was shoving the boxes in her halter top, which was already bulging with coins. She opened the halter top up and I poured in all the loose coins I had until her top was full. Coins were spilling on the floor and I tried to grab them as they fell. I put my two hands together and caught coins rolling from the money fountain. My hands filled up in a minute and the half dollars spilled all over like a 4-aces slot machine pull. Coins were everywhere. I started filling the grocery bag with boxes.

"Hey," I said. "How many can you cram in your panty hose?"

I wondered if there were guards watching us from a little surveillance room. I remembered there were cameras everywhere and figured everything was being recorded. As soon as I realized I was being recorded, I did what everyone in that situation does, I gave the finger. Since I didn't know where the camera was, I did a 360 while giving the finger.

Well, they had probably seen Kim and me loading up the coins. They were going to be coming after us. I figured one guard was telling the other guard to look for Beaver Cleaver's mom.

That's when I heard something unfamiliar. "Okay, people, the party's over." Everyone booed. Kim and I looked out the window and saw a guard had taken control of the DJ booth. I figured they were going to try and clear the place out. The music was turned off and the guard spoke on the mic.

"Okay, everyone, let's all head outta here and over to Civic Center. That's where the party is," the guard said.

The crowd booed, this time with ultimate vitriol. One person yelled, "Turn up the music!"

The guard said, "There's free beer at Civic Center. And vodka!" Damn, the guard was using the same trick I had tried on Minnie Cooper. The Clean and Sober gays booed and held up their banner.

"And the mayor's getting his nipple pierced," the guard said. Seeing Gavin get a tit pierce was kind of tempting, but no one took the bait. "And they've got pumps in size 10 and up - half off!" Wow. This guard was pulling out the big guns.

I could see Lisa Box after the guard said there was a sale on oversized heels. She fingered her necklace. Even though I was pretty far away, I could see she was pondering making a break for it. I imagined A Dyke on a Bike yelling, "What's a pumps?"

The guard was pissed and gave up. "Ah, forget it," he said. You could hear the anger in his voice. "But you can bet every single one of you will be frisked on the way out!"

Well, that was it. The crowd got excited and they all made an orderly rush to the exit and properly lined up. Cheer SF started cheering, "I'm Frisky, so Frisk Me!" We could hear them all the way to the second or third floor, wherever we were. Everyone was eager for a frisking. The guard shook his head but headed to the front of the line.

The guards were frisking people as they exited, and I saw them finish with this one guy and he hurried back in line to be frisked again. There was a guy wearing only leather shorts, but he took the guard's hands and rubbed them up and down his pecs, forcing the guard to frisk his bare chest.

Kim and I had stuffed all the coins we could handle into our dresses. "Let's get out of here," I said. We headed for the hallway, then saw two guards. We ducked under a machine, but we could hear them.

"What did they take?" one guard asked.

"They made a big mess, but it doesn't look like they took anything," the other guard said. "I don't get it."

"What about Mrs. Cleaver?"

"No sign."

I was right. They had ID-ed me and they were looking for me. I pointed to the stacks of boxed coins, and Kim and I hid behind it. "They're coming for us," I said.

"Where's Chad?" Kim asked.

"He's long gone. We need to scram."

We started to leave, and I wanted to try and go the back way, so we wouldn't get frisked. We both must have weighed an extra hundred pounds and were jingling with every step while I dragged the stuffed grocery bag. I pointed the way I wanted to go. We moved through the racks of boxed coins, slowly but surely. "Be quiet," I said. It was just too tempting. I told Kim, "I'm gonna take one of these racks." They were on wheels. It should be easy. I pulled one of the racks and tipped the whole damn thing over and made a ton of noise. I saw the look on Kim's face; it was pure fear.

"What's wrong?" I said.

"I'm stuck," Kim said.

"Whaddya mean you're stuck?" I said. I didn't have time to play around.

"My foot is stuck," she said.

"Chew it off," I said.

"Har-de-har-har," Kim said. The rack of boxed coins had fallen on her leg and she was trapped. She tried pulling her foot out, but it wouldn't budge. She couldn't pull her foot out of the shoe either. Her foot was wedged in there like a vise. "They're coming," she said. "We're meat."

"Is it broken?" I said.

"No, it's just stuck." We both struggled with the rack. I pulled Kim, but the only thing that moved was her arm. The rack was just too heavy. I thought maybe I could pull all the coins out of the rack, then try and pick it up. But that would make so much noise… and if I didn't get the coins completely out of the way, I would end up doing it twice. That's when we heard the guards talking again. They were coming! The guards!

Kim pulled at her leg, trying to get free. "C'mon!" she said. "We can't get caught!"

And that was when something snapped in my head. It sounded like a harp string, breaking. A pleasant sound that ended with a sorrowful thud. And that's when I did it. I freaked out. I looked Kim in the eye, and I screamed, "You're on your own, dude!" And I ran, dragging the grocery bag full of boxed coins with me.

Chapter 21 – The Girl's Gotta Have It

I ran down the stairs, back to the lobby, then exploded out of the gigantic gold door. It set off alarms, but so what? There were only those handful of guards and they were still frisking people. I knew I could get away and I ran. But I had run out a door that left me stranded in the back of the building. I was going to have to get back in or walk around to the front or something. First, I needed to catch my breath and collect my wits.

There were some trumpet vines growing nearby and for all the chaos and danger around me, I saw a hummingbird dipping its long beak into one of the red flowers. This was a good sign. Chad had said the hummingbird was a good sign. I pointed at the hummer. I watched the rapid quiver of the bird's wings and it made me feel okay. I calmed down. I spoke directly to the tiny bird. "Thank you, little hummingbird! Now I know it's gonna be all right. Everything's gonna be all –" and right then a raven swooped in, snatched up the hummingbird, and flew off with it, flapping its beautiful black wings and holding the tiny bird in its mouth.

My good sign just got eaten! Now what? And what about no natural enemies? I thought. No natural enemies! Damn that Chad! He didn't know shit! And there were guards out to get me and I was wasting time, standing by the fence, talking to a bird. One that just made a tasty lunch for a naughty raven.

I guess I knew I was disoriented at that point, but one thing about being disoriented is you think everything's okay and you think that you're functioning normally. But let's be real. At that point, I didn't know what I was doing. I went back toward the building and leaned against the bars on one of the lower windows.

I turned and saw my reflection. I was a mess. The wig was crooked, and hair was sticking out all over the place. The makeup was smeared like cream cheese on a bagel, my dress was ripped, and it looked like I had gotten engine grease on it. But one thing was still perfect: those pearls. Those June Cleaver pearls, left by my mother, and only worn twice. First at that stupid prom where Ted got jumped and I abandoned him. I touched the pearls and thought how once again I had abandoned a friend to save my own ass. Those pearls. They had so much wound up in them. I stroked them again, feeling the string around my neck. And all of a sudden, I grabbed them with a decisive yank, and pulled. The string holding them together had been strong and Chad had said they were double strung or double tied or something, but they were old so the string broke and the pearls that had been tied together for decades were now free to take advantage of their unplanned escape. One of the pearls rolled off the ledge, and I grabbed for it, but there was no way I could catch it. Then the others flew by, and I watched them one by one, pinging, bouncing, flying free. They ricocheted off the concrete, and they rolled down the back steps, jumping into the dirt, disappearing from view. My poor little brain was misfiring in so many ways. Wait! I thought, like I could will the pearls back to me. That pearl necklace was the only connection I had with my mother! Dang! I grabbed at empty air and called, "Mom!"

I watched the last few beads roll from the concrete ledge into the brush. I opened my palm. I had caught two. Well, it was something. I put the two beads in my bra, and I got up. I started walking toward the giant gold door. If I was lucky, I could get back in. I wasn't sure what I was going to do. Was I surrendering? Is that what I was doing? I think I was closer to the front entrance now, I wasn't even sure. But I stumbled, in my kitten heels, with my ripped and dirty dress, my fucked-up wig, and half of someone else's tiara that was stuck in the hair, to the back entrance. The door hadn't fully closed, but only a crack was open. Bit by bit, I forced my fingers in until I could get a grip and pull it. It weighed a ton, but I heaved the mother open and I went back into the lobby, still dragging the grocery bag. A guard was now standing nearby. He saw me. Well, I was about as obvious as a car crash, so there was no way he couldn't see me.

"It's June Cleaver! Get her!" the guard yelled.

I tried to steady myself, and I just stood there looking at him. Then all of a sudden my five-foot, two-inch self charged toward the guard, and I mowed him down. For whatever reason, my body had taken over where my brain had failed. In my head, I had decided to do what was right this time. I was going to protect my friend, no matter what it cost me physically or monetarily. It was more important to save Kim than it was to pull off this caper. This may have been the first time in my life I had done the right thing. But while I love to ponder a situation, roll it around in my head, and consider it, conducting some self-congratulatory patting of my own back, my head was spent. The battered body had taken over and was making all the choices.

I raced back to where I had deserted Kim. And by race, I mean I kind of hurried as best I could because I was really running out of fuel at this point and I was sort of shuffling along in the kitten heels. I was sort of scraping the shoes on the floor and dragging myself up the steps. I could feel that the panty hose had slipped down, about a half foot from my crotch. If this was what being feminine was about, I hated it!

I was completely operating on adrenaline and what was left of the three cups of joe I'd had that morning. The shoes stunk. My heels kept slipping out of them and I was so used to wearing sneakers. "Oh, what I'd give for a pair of Doc Martins right now!" I said, and I didn't even care who heard me. Let them find me, let them try and get me. I was on a mission!

I hid for a moment. There were advantages to being small. I ducked behind some machinery and watched. Two of the guards were there, still trying to lift the cart and get Kim's foot out. Apparently, her tootsies were really wedged in there. I looked around. I saw a rainbow flag on a pole that someone had left behind. Then the guards got Kim's foot out and she was moaning about how it hurt. The guard I had knocked over came running up to the other guards and seemed to be filling them in on what had happened. The guards were holding Kim and were getting ready to cuff her.

I picked up the gay flag on a pole. It had a pointy end, but I figured it wasn't really sharp, but I didn't need it to be. All I needed was to look like a nutjob and we all knew at this point, I didn't need much help. I held the flagpole horizontally and yelled, "Hands off that dyke!"

The guard that held Kim dropped his hands and stared at Kim. "I thought it was a man!" he said. Kim's glasses were all sideways and her hair was a mess like mine. The top of her gown still bulged with half dollars, but every time she moved a few would fall out and hit the floor. Two guards grabbed her again.

One of the guards was coming at me. He had his hand on his gun, but it was still in the holster. He held his other arm out at me. "Put that down," he said. "We don't want to hurt you."

"Too late! I'm already hurt!" I said. "And you're no match for my determination. My sintillating – is it sintillating? Or skintillating? Oh, I know, my scintillating creativity. My plucky grit." This was turning into every crappy crime movie I'd ever seen. The cops were negotiating with the nutjob, it's just that this time, I was the nutjob. And, in the movies, this always ended in one of two ways. Either the nutjob surrendered or the nutjob got shot dead. The nutjob never won. "Did you ever see *Dog Day Afternoon?*" I asked the cop.

Then I saw him slowly draw his gun. I would like to point out for the sake of social justice, if I had been black, I would have already been shot about half an hour before this point. But I wasn't dead yet.

"Okay, forget the plucky grit," I said. I held the flagpole up, and all of a sudden it was a lightning rod, a pole of power. I could be feminine, well, maybe, and the feminine could be strong. "I call upon the energy of the goddess…!" I said. "Um...anybody know the name of a goddess? Wait - I know one! I call upon the energy of Xena, Warrior Princess!" For those that don't know, Xena, Warrior Princess, was a TV show, though that cannot diminish the fact that she was a kick-ass warrior.

I heard one guard say to the other, "You're right, boss. We should have called mental health."

"Okay, coin boy," I said, "get ready for a world of hurt!" With a blood curdling scream, I hoisted the flag above my head, and just like a pole vaulter in drag, I ran, full speed, right at the guards. Okay, blame it on slightly poor depth perception, but before I was anywhere near them, I slammed the pole into the wall, knocked the wind out of myself, and fell on my ass. It was an absolute miss. The guards rushed over to help me. I was flat on my back on the floor and just like a cartoon I saw little stars and could hear tweety birds. When the guards were half a step away, I bolted up and yelled, "RUN!!!"

I was up. I don't know how I got up, but I was up, and I was running, and I grabbed Kim's arm and pulled her and we both bolted for the exit.

"You came back!" Kim said.

"Shut up and let's get out of here," I said as we ran.

"I thought I was gonna get beaten down, like your prom date," Kim said.

I held my fist up to her and said, "Shut up, or you will be!"

We ran and my brain wasn't even connected at that point, so we just ran. Kim was dragging the foot that had been trapped. We got out of the Mint, running from the front then onto Hermann Street and toward the waiting Scion.

My hands were shaking, but somehow, I was able to open the door and I jumped into the driver's seat. I fired Baby up. Kim jumped into the passenger side. "Gun it!" she yelled.

I pulled out of the tight parking spot, but it took a couple of tries since I didn't want to scratch the bumper; but in a minute, I was on the street. I hit the gas and pulled a 360. This is no small feat on a San Francisco street.

"What was that?" Kim yelled.

"Oh. I always wanted to do that," I said. "Cool, huh?"

What wasn't cool was that the guards were on our tail. One on foot and two in a car. Again, I hadn't thought this through, so I was driving, but I didn't know where.

"Go down Guerrero!" Kim yelled.

"Guerrero?!? It's so slow! Plus, Dolores is much more scenic." I was facing west now and drove down Hermann to Church. I waited behind the stop sign and signaled to make a left.

"What're you doing?"

"Waiting for the pedestrian," I said.

"Go!!!" Kim yelled. "Just go!"

I turned onto Church, and I got into the track lane which is always a mistake and might even be illegal on this street. In the rearview I saw one of the guards leaning from the car. He fired.

"Oh shit!" I said.

"Omigod!" Kim screamed.

Like I said, I hadn't thought this through, and while I had thought about guards and weapons, I had never thought GUN or BULLETS. He fired again and hit the rear passenger tire. I hit the gas, but Baby fishtailed and came to a stop, sideways, on the Church Street tracks, right before we crossed Market.

Kim was caressing the dash. "Go, Baby, go!" she coaxed. "Go Baby, please!" But Baby was down for the count.

The guards were out of the car and coming for us. SFPD rolled up and parked on the other side of Church. The cops got out of the car and were coming too, and they had their guns drawn. I think this is when I just stopped breathing.

The guard had his gun pointed at me, both hands on the gun, and I knew that meant he could take me out any minute. "Put your hands up!" he yelled. "Come out! Put your hands up!"

I opened the door, just a bit. I was getting ready to slide out. That's when I saw two lights coming around the corner from Duboce. Yeah, it was the "J" and check this – it was going ten times faster than ever! Yeah, 50 miles per hour! I stared at the lights.

We both still sat in Baby. I turned to Kim and said, "Get out."

"No. No!" she said. "You go. Go without me!"

"Get out," I repeated.

"I'll never leave her!" Kim cried.

I pushed the door open with my foot. I slid out of Baby with my hands up. Then I dunno, it was the body again, acting without a brain and in my case, that may have been a good thing. I ran. I ran to the other side of the Scion, and I grabbed the door open, and I pulled Kim out. I don't know how the hell I pulled her out since she's bigger than I am, but I pulled her out and dragged her to the sidewalk.

We stood there, looking like complete assholes, with the smeared ruby red lipstick and the stupid heels and the idiotic dresses, two sorry dropouts from the clown college of womanhood and we watched.

"Stupid "J"! Now it comes!" I said. I tried to push Kim's face away. "Don't look," I said. "It's going to be awful!" That, of course made Kim want to look. She pushed my hand out of the way.

The "J" couldn't stop. It rang the bell and hit the horn, but it couldn't stop. The "J" broadsided Baby, crushing her beyond recognition. The sweet, beautiful Baby was gone.

Kim collapsed to her knees. She was crying. "My Baby! My Baby!"

One of the cops was standing there and she asked, "Was there a baby in there?"

Around this time, my brain was coming back online. I thought for a moment and I said, "Yes." I wasn't trying to stall for time or anything, I just liked the idea of wasting the cop's time.

The cop ran to the Scion. The "J" train was halfway across Market with a smashed-up silver SUV stuck to the front. Man, if there anything worse than robbery, it was this. I had stalled traffic. On Market Street, no less. On Pride weekend. I knew the penalties for that would cut deep.

I helped Kim get up. Her face was tear and mascara stained. "Baby...!" she gasped. Then Kim looked at me. "You saved me," she said. "You saved me twice today. You're not a complete jackass. You're a friend."

"Who you callin' friend?" I said. Then I remembered friend didn't mean bitch to Kim. It meant friend. I hadn't gotten my fat rolls of uncut bills, but for once, I had done the right thing. "Oh," I said. "Thanks."

And in that moment, I had one of those insights

like at the end of *The Grinch Who Stole Christmas*. For once, my endless rumination resulted in knowledge. I couldn't beat drag queens at the girl game, and I was never going to be cute or femmy or helpless. I wasn't any of those things. But that day, I had discovered one thing that I had that might be feminine. Compassion. Maybe two. Friendship. This was a lot of musing that happened in about ten seconds.

Then two police officers were there, and they cuffed us, and I was telling the officer that the cuffs were way too tight when the Mint guards ran over. They used the real metal cuffs, not the plastic ones, and they were heavy, and they pinched.

"Did they get anything?" one of the police officers asked.

The guard was angry. "Not much," he said. "But they touched a lot of coins."

I guessed this guy was a big germaphobe. I mean, who cared if we touched the coins. "So what?" I said. "They were only half dollars."

The guard started yelling at us and he spit when he spoke, and it was really gross. "Those weren't half-dollars!" he said. "They're silver proof commemorative coins."

"Ah shit!" I said. I had no idea what they must have been worth, but it was more than fifty cents.

"Uncirculated, until you touched them!"

"Did they get the gold bars?"

Gold Bars? I looked at Kim and she looked at me. We had broken into the Fort Knox of the West and instead of becoming rich, we'd had a dance party. Well, at least it had been a pretty good dance party.

"No," the guard said, and he started brushing himself off, like he was trying to wipe us off, I guess.

The cop started to read us our Miranda rights and though I have the right to remain silent, I have rarely used it. The cop said them just like every cop show on TV. "You have the right to remain silent. Anything you say can and will be used against you..."

I stopped him and said, "I do have something to say."

But the cop didn't listen to me and just continued with the Miranda rights. "You have the right to an attorney," he said. "If you cannot afford an attorney, one will be provided for you."

But another cop had heard me and said, "Then say it."

The cops had their hands on me, and I was cuffed,

and I tried to stand up straight. I prepared to speak. I cleared my throat. I would have liked to have held my index finger in the air to emphasize the import of my statement, but I couldn't, because of the cuffs. Finally, I was ready to speak.

"Say it!" the cop yelled.

I breathed in all the air I could and shouted, "Go Giants!"

Chapter 22 – Don't Rain on my Parade

I learned later that we made the evening news. Lynne got out from the panty hose and saw us that night from the safety of her living room, drinking a glass of wine. One of the local news stations carried it, we didn't make the national, but after the parade footage there was a small story about us. When Lynne told me, she imitated the news announcer. "...estimated to be a crowd of nearly three-quarter of a million spectators. There were a handful of arrests including an unsuccessful attempt to break into the U.S. Mint by two unlikely female impersonators."

Chad, who had disappeared on us, saw it too. He told me that night he was pretty wasted and was getting banged from behind. And while he was getting banged, he was watching the news, not for news, but just for pictures of the parade. All he talked about though was the mugshots. "Your mugshot was frightening!" he said. "Yelp! As a makeup artiste, I've moved into my cubist period! Please don't let anyone know I had anything to do with that monstrosity!"

Daneetra saw it too. But what she saw was Tom Ammiano. She said Tommy was complaining, something like "These two are an insult to gays everywhere. On parade day, in drag..." Well, I don't know about you, but what could be better than being shamed by Tom Ammiano? Dammit, I was almost famous. Daneetra did a pretty good imitation of him: "...and, to top it off, they couldn't even get any money! Scandalous! Shame! Shame!" Daneetra saw the mugshots too, and she said she got a good laugh out of them. That was cool cause at that time in my life, I sure could have used a good laugh.

Chapter 23 – Live Free...

Well, about two years later, there I was giving a lecture at The Herbst Theatre. The place was packed, all 928 seats filled, and there were some people standing up too. I was at the front, at a podium. I looked about the same, hair uncombed, jeans, and a t-shirt that read "Another Angry Bitch for Peace," you know, business as usual. Except, I had gotten my ears pierced, and I wore pearl earrings. Yeah, they were made from those two pearls I had salvaged.

And one thing that had changed was I now loved the sound of my own voice because it was making me money. I was wrapping things up. "And in closing, I'd like to say...." I held this stack of index cards I used to deliver every speech. All the cards were blank, but it gave the impression that I had prepared. I thumbed through them and "found" the blank card I was looking for. "Ah!" I said. "And then, well, er, um, in close. Ing. In closing, if yer yerself, then it'll all work out. If you, uh, live free... um... Live Free or Else!" And with that, the crowd jumped to their feet and went ballistic with applause.

I was done, another lecture for the books and, speaking of books, I was in the lobby, autographing a few hundred. There were stacks of them. The cover had my mug on the front, smack on a three-dollar bill. The text across my silly face read: *Live Free or Else!* by A.J. Billingsley. Someone was ringing up sales. I held up a copy of the book and posed for a picture.

"Good thing SOMEONE can write these," I said, and I carelessly flipped the book back into the pile. I grabbed someone's wrist and checked their watch. "Oop. Gotta go. Baby shower!"

I got up, walked down Van Ness, and headed west on Market Street. It was a crisp afternoon. From the side of my eye, I saw a ride roll up with a bunch of rowdy males. Uh oh, I thought. Here comes trouble. There were a lot of them in the car and I prepared in case they tried to jump me.

One guy stuck his head out the window and yelled at me. "Hey, aren't you the gay girl who tried to rob the Mint?"

I was caught off guard. It wasn't what I expected. "Uh... yeah," I said.

"You almost got it, girl! Nice try. Me and my boys are gonna hit the Fed!"

"Good luck!" I yelled.

One of the other guys in the car yelled, "Not me. I'm getting my MBA!"

"We love you!" the first guy yelled, and they drove off.

Man, I had arrived. I was a minor celebrity, one with a hint of notoriety. Who knew life could be so good? I continued walking down Market Street. It was a disaster and that meant there was always something to look at. Homeless people slept in dirty sleeping bags, people were passed out, bottles in hand, drag queens walked down the street, there was a group of cute young Asian boys who could make a boy band, and a man who wore an incomprehensible sandwich board sign, something about Jesus or one of his friends, I couldn't really tell. It was sort of a Statue of Liberty West scene: bring me your mohawked, your rehabbed, your certifiably insane. I breathed it all in. This was my City.

I called out to no one: "It's a world of freaks and I'm the jester!" I kept talking to myself, mostly so I would fit in with the crowd. "Wow. This way is so much better than just bein' a crook. For one thing, I didn't have to roll all those coins!"

A homeless guy came up to me and asked, "Spare change?"

"As a matter of fact, I do have change to spare. You see, if you learn to embrace your fabulosity, the good, the bad, and, in your case, the ugly, you can truly change and transform the world."

The homeless guy said, "I meant money, friend."

"Who you callin'...? Oh." I realized he wouldn't know what I was talking about. "You mean loose change. Here ya go, Pops. Knock yourself out. Get yerself a Budweiser suitcase." I opened my wallet which was exploding with bills and I gave him a ten.

I finally got to Kim's new restaurant. It was on Market, near the Castro. Kim's parents were there and so was The Mouse. Yeah, Brenda had waited for Kim to get out of the hole. And, yeah, Brenda had moved in with Kim and taken my spot at the Dolores Street house. Brenda was a stupid friend!

Pink banners were all over the place. "Welcome Baby!" they read. There was a cake and presents. Kim and Brenda were all over each other. It made me want to puke. Lynne waved a crystal wand over the couple. I really needed a drink.

"Finally! Today's the day!" Kim said.

"I told ya it would all work out," I said.

Kim looked at me and smiled. "That was the stupidest, smartest thing we ever did," she said.

"Ah!" I said. "The notoriety! It's catapulted us into the middle class!"

"Isn't it amazing?" Lynne said. "You embraced the feminine and everything turned around."

"Nah," I said. "I just got lucky. That, and this country's insatiable feeding frenzy for scandal! I mean, look, I got ten years. I only had to do six months."

"Did you get out for good behavior?" someone I didn't know asked.

"No, apparently I was just driving everyone crazy and they wanted me to leave. But while I was there, I had a great time! I look great in orange, I got an hour of exercise I wouldn't do, and that prison chow was terrific! Three meals a day!"

I had some great ideas when I got out. For starters, I contacted the U.S. Mint and suggested they create a coin set that commemorated me breaking in. They were not real hep on this idea, so I didn't pitch my ideas for the t-shirts and snow globes. Well, so what. The stupid Mint didn't even have a gift shop! Luckily, the book deal came along.

And then it was time for the new baby to arrive. Kim got all choked up and grabbed The Mouse. We stood outside and a new Scion rolled up to the curb. This one was Super White, and it was a stunner. Everyone rushed up to greet the new Baby and complimented the glossy paint job, the interior, and the new car smell.

Chad was there, wearing a hoochiefied outfit that he must have snagged from some sort of tramp town shop. It was leopard print, and like camo, I've never quite understood the attraction to leopard print. This was a pleather leopard print mini dress that barely covered his ass. He was wearing a beauty pageant sash and had a guy hanging on him.

"Do you strap that thing on your chest every day?" I asked.

"Yes!" Chad said. "Oh, you mean my sash!" He ran his hand across the sash. "I thought you meant my new boyfriend-slash-campaign manager, Lance."

Chad's new boyfriend, Lance, was buff and black. He wore leather chaps, leather hat, and no shirt. He had a mustache. I guess he was ready and waiting just in case the Village People needed a new singer.

We all went back inside, and Kim and Brenda sat while friends showered them with presents. Kim opened the first one. "A steering wheel cover!" she said. Then another. It was a car bra. "Her first bra!" Kim said.

Lance held a small teddy bear. He looked out the window at the Scion. He tossed the teddy bear in the trash. Lance shrugged and looked at me. He said, "I thought it was going to be…." He rocked his arms indicating a baby.

Chad looked and him and said, "Oh, honey, we're gay, but we're not stupid!"

"Correction," I said. "We're stupid. But we're not THAT stupid!"

Chad said, "Yeah!" Then he looked at Lance and said, "So Mr. Leatherman." And he pretended to pick up a phone. "Ring, ring. What's that? Oh, it's a booty call!"

Lance put his arms around Chad and said, "I'll get it."

"You bet you will," Chad said, and they went off together.

They were still opening presents when I interrupted. "I got something too!" I said. I signaled for Kim to follow me and everyone walked outside to the side of the restaurant. There was a sheet pinned on the wall. I ceremoniously pulled down the sheet and there on the wall, were spray painted the word everyone in San Francisco dreams of: RESERVED.

"Omigod! Omigod!" Kim said and she fell to her

knees again. "I can't believe it. A parking spot!" Tears welled up in Kim's eyes. "A parking spot," she said again, and she was at a loss for words. "A, a, I, I can't believe it! Thank you!"

"Getting arrested was the most brilliant thing we've ever done!" I said.

Next to the spot for Baby was a new red Harley. That spot was reserved too, but it was reserved for me. I jumped on the Harley and took off. I pulled up in front of a house in the Duboce Triangle. Daneetra was at the curb. She put on a helmet and hopped on the bike.

We were tooling around in the Civic Center, and I drove the bike right up on the plaza. I drove up to the flag that read "Live Free or Die." "Look," I said. "Whaddya think of that?" I asked.

The flag waved in the wind. "Live Free or Die," Daneetra read. She gave it a big smirk and said, "I bet that flag was made by somebody who owned slaves."

"Yeah, that would figure, wouldn't it? Par for the course in the good old U.S. of A.D.D.," I said. I revved up the Harley and I nodded toward City Hall. "Wanna get hitched?" I asked.

"I'm not a horse," Daneetra said.

"Okay. Wanna get married?" I asked. "It's legal now. At least I think it is."

There was a long pause and finally Daneetra said, "No."

"Okay," I said. "Wanna get Chinese?"

"Now you're talking," Daneetra said.

We zoomed away. I drove by a meter maid and kicked at her. The meter maid kicked back. We zoomed past the ornate carvings, the commanding dome, the filigree gold trim of City Hall, and rode off into the Sunset... District that was, for some sizzling rice soup and mushu pork.

Also by BK Wells

Nothing To Fear

What happens when the dumbest guy on the planet becomes President?

We'd have **Nothing To Fear**, of course! Junior Worthy is dumb as dog shit, but he's Vice President. Worthy is unqualified and uninformed, and when he lands in the top spot, Congressman Tip Murphy doesn't want to be his VP, fired Press Secretary Jim Donaldson is out to kill him, and San Francisco mom, Kennedy Jefferson, serves as a willing, but unprepared advisor. Except for that Trump thing, US politics just couldn't be nuttier than this crazy Capitol romp!

CPSIA information can be obtained
at www.ICGtesting.com
Printed in the USA
LVHW080528230622
721884LV00002B/135